The Expedition

Maxwell Pearl

Preface

The Casitian Universe is set in our galaxy, in particular, the stars of the Orion Arm. There are many intelligent species in the Orion Arm, and many star systems are tied together by a series of wormholes that were created by a species that is no longer in the galaxy. The wormholes are maintained by a species named the Keeelo.

Five thousand years ago, ten thousand human beings were taken from earth, from twelve different regions, to provide slave labor for the Tud'scla, a species later banned from any contact with the Galactic Community. Humans served the Tud'scla for two thousand years, and then were freed, and given the planet "Casiti" to live on. Returning the now 50 million humans to Earth was considered by the Galactic Community to be too disruptive to primitive Terran culture.

Casitians are completely mixed-race, since they are made up of humans from all over Earth, and were forced to interbreed, as the Tud'scla elevated hybrid vigor to a religion. The society that humans evolved on Casiti was nonviolent, egalitarian, communitarian, and environmentally sustainable.

In the first book of the series, "The Casitians Return" these humans return publicly in 2011 to be reunited with humans on Earth. However, each 20 Casitian years since the Casitian year 102 there has been a secret expedition to Earth to get information about what was happening on Earth, and how it was developing. This book is the story of the 32nd such expedition, started in Casitian year 742, which was Earth year 1859.

Chapter 1

Expedition Log 742.4.1. Student: Jam'elo z Kadarin. Date: 115 Paqn 742

My AI has been monitoring the listening devices placed all over the area where I'll start my travels, known as the state of Minnesota. I have been looking for an appropriate town to begin my explorations. The plan is the same as for all previous expeditions - to find ways to serve in the capacity of a healer, while observing the culture and technology. In the past, that has been a good strategy for observation - but it may provide some complexities in this particular context.

The land area that is now called North America has undergone much change since the last expedition in 723. We have not visited this continent at all since the fateful expedition of 702, when one of the students was gravely injured in an unexpected violent conflict. It became clear then that the physical appearance of Casitians was going to be far too unusual for us to be able to blend in here, so we focused our attention elsewhere on Reit'al during the last expedition.

I successfully argued that a Casitian could be able to operate in some areas of North America now, and that it would be instructive to understand the experience of someone who looks like me within that context. Her'ellen is a little worried about my safety, but I have no such concerns. I don't think that I'll be in any more danger than any other Casitian student in the past, and our safeguards will be enough to keep me from being injured.

I identified a town called Saint Paul as my first stop. It is a large town, the capital of the geographic territory. I will find a hospital where I can begin work.

Attached to this log are my analyses of the data from the listening devices around Minnesota. A short summary: the population of the area is about 170,000. There are a large number of people who moved here after the last AI survey in 722, when an indigenous population was present. That population has been largely replaced by the immigrants from the northeastern part of the continent. The technology here is comparable to technology available elsewhere on this continent.

Saint Paul, Minnesota, 117 Paqn, 742/April 13, 1859

Jam'elo turned around, even though he knew he wouldn't see the shuttle leave. He heard the rushing sound and felt the stiff breeze it kicked up as it was taking off. He turned back around to see the first group of houses in the distance, on the edge of the city. He had a long walk ahead of him.

It was a clear day, and warm to Jam'elo. It was only early spring here, and he could see flowers of very unfamiliar types starting to bloom. He could tell that spring was going to be a much more rapid and boisterous affair than it was on Casiti. As he walked, he could see the small farmhouses, and varied domestic animals grazing. It was quiet mostly, save for the sounds of birds singing.

He had a small bag with him with his clothing, appropriate for the setting, his medical equipment, his recorder for logs, and a few other things. He expected to spend a few months in Saint Paul, then travel to two or three other places before the end of the expedition next year at the end of Musb. That would be about four Earth years of exploration and research. He was eager to see what lay ahead.

There were few people in the streets this morning. He heard a clop clop sound coming up behind him, and he turned around to see a large animal that he knew was called a "horse". There was an older man sitting on top of the horse.

The man asked, "Where are you headed, boy?"

Jam'elo answered, "Hello. I'm on my way to the center of town. I have some business there." The first thing he needed to do was exchange a small bit of gold into local currency. Then he would find his way to a hospital.

"What kind of business?" Jam'elo thought that the man's demeanor was strange. His tone seemed hostile. The man shifted his horse to block Jam'elo's way. Jam'elo wanted to be friendly, but careful.

"I've been traveling quite a lot. I'm a doctor. I'm on my way to the hospital."

Even though Jam'elo didn't know the man, he could tell the man was suspicious.

"Where are you from?"

"I am from far away—not from this continent."

"Boy, you look more like you came up from the South."

Jam'elo wanted to end this conversation and move on. He wasn't quite sure what this man would do next.

"I didn't come from the South. I need to keep walking; I hope you have a nice day." Jam'elo started to walk around the horse, whose head followed him as he circled it. At first, he thought the man would prevent him from walking on, but the man let him go. After a few paces, Jam'elo looked back, and saw the man staring at him. He turned and kept walking.

As he continued his way into the center of town, there were more people walking about, and he garnered quite a number of stares. He finally made his way to the gold merchant—an obvious facade let him know where it was—and he walked in. There were several men sitting behind counters with scales, and only a few customers. He made his way to one of the clerks.

"Hello. I have some gold I need to exchange."

"Well, let me look at it."

Jam'elo had been given several ounces of gold for exchange. He gave a small pouch with the first bit of gold to the clerk. The clerk emptied it onto a scale. He looked at Jam'elo.

"That's 2.5 ounces of gold. That's worth 43 dollars and 20 cents today. That's a lot of money, boy. Where did you get this gold?"

Jam'elo was mystified by all of this suspicion. He couldn't understand what warranted it. And he couldn't figure out why this man, and the man on the horse, thought he was underage.

"I'm a traveler from far away, and I was told that gold was the best thing to exchange for money once I got out West."

"How far away is your home?"

"Very far. I'm not from this continent."

The man laughed, and said, "You surely talk strangely, but I find that hard to believe."

Jam'elo spread his hands. "Believe whatever you'd like. Will you exchange the gold?"

The clerk got up from his chair, and went into the back, and returned with a man wearing a different sort of attire. It looked to Jam'elo to be much more formal, with more layers. And it was darkly colored. He wondered if the man got hot in those clothes.

This new man asked, "What's your name?"

"My name is Jam'elo Kadarin."

"What kind of name is that?"

"I'm from far away from here."

"Have you ever seen the city of New York?" Jam'elo had spent a few days in New York quite recently. The expedition had a training facility there where everyone went first.

"Yes, I've been to New York."

"What's that new big park they are building in...?"

"It's called 'The Central Park' in Manhattan"

The man looked thoughtful, then said to his clerk, "Exchange the gold."

Jam'elo took the money, and walked out of the merchant, in search for somewhere to stay. It ended up being a very frustrating experience. The first and second places he went men at the door refused to let him enter at all. The third place was a small, older hotel, where he had to walk through a saloon to get to the proprietor to find out about the room. Before he even got halfway through the saloon, his way was blocked by several men, and it appeared that he would be the catalyst for some sort of violent outbreak, so he turned around and left quickly.

He walked down to the fourth place he had been told about. It was a large house close to the outskirts of town. It looked quite run-down, compared to the others he had seen. The surface of the building was flaking off, and the steps and porch looked like they needed repair.

No sign suggested that it was a rooming house, but there were many people coming and going. He walked up the steps onto the porch, and peered in the door, to see a woman behind a desk, staring at him. He walked over to her.

"I'm looking to rent a room for a while."

She shook her head. "I'm sorry, but we don't rent any rooms to coloreds."

"Excuse me? I'm not what you think…"

"You sure look like one."

Jam'elo sighed. "I do need lodging, and I'm not familiar with this city. Do you have any suggestions?"

"I'd try out on the West Side. There are some people who might rent you a room."

"Thank you."

Jam'elo left and walked toward the west side of town. It was getting late, and he hoped he would be able to find a place to stay for a while. This was outside of his expectation based on the experiences of other Casitian students in the past, although this was a very different context than any Casitians had encountered before. A night or two out in the open wouldn't kill him, but he was frustrated, and felt close to giving up. He'd been able to obtain some fruit from a vendor, but he had been viewed with so much suspicion that he feared going into one of those places where they served food.

He saw a man with a dark skin tone selling a variety of items from his cart and thought that it would be a good idea to ask him for advice on finding a place to stay.

"Hello there."

"Hey. I got some tinctures, here—want some? I got fresh honey, too."

"Actually, I'm looking for a place to stay."

The man shook his head. "A place to stay? You gotsta be careful 'round here."

"I haven't been able to find a place."

"I ain't surprised. Look, my brother's family has a room dey rent, and last I heard it was empty. I sure dey rent it to you. Dey de Chisslers. Dey live over dere on dat street two streets down."

"What's the name of the street?"

He laughed. "It don't have a name. It's de one with de yellowish house on de corner. Just go down a couple houses and ask someone."

"Thank you very much."

Jam'elo walked down to the street, and was directed by an older, very friendly woman to the Chissler house. It was a smaller house than some on the block, but it clearly had been well taken care of. There were flowers planted in the front, and the outside looked a lot newer and brighter than many he had passed. He knocked, and a woman answered. She was tall and was wearing a simple blue dress with an apron.

"May I help you?"

"Yes, my name is Jam'elo. Your relative who sells from the cart told me that you have a room to rent. I'm looking for a place to stay."

"Yes, we have a room. The room and board is two dollars. If you want to help around the house, the room'll be one-fifty. We're almost finished painting, and we could use some help with that."

"Painting? I don't know what that is, but I can help."

The woman frowned at him. "How long you gonna stay?"

"I'm not sure—possibly a couple of months."

"Well, I need to talk to my husband, and he's out working now. He be back soon. Come in... Jameelo, and have a seat. Are you hungry?"

"Thanks, yes, I am."

He followed her into the modest dwelling, and she directed him to sit at the table in the kitchen. He noticed the primitive cooking implements. The inside of the house looked as well taken care of as the outside.

"My name is Dina. My husband's name is Lou."

"Nice to meet you, Dina."

"I got a pot of pea soup. Want some?"

Jam'elo had no idea what pea soup was, but he figured it was good. Everything he'd eaten so far was good to his taste.

"Sounds fine. Thank you."

She placed a big bowl in front of him, and the smell of the soup was wonderful.

"Thank you so much." He started to spoon the soup into his mouth.

"Where you from, Jameelo? You talk strange."

"I'm from far away, not on this continent."

"From where?"

"It's called Casiti. You've never heard of it. It's very, very far away."

"Why are you here?"

"I wanted to travel and explore. I wanted to learn about the people here."

Dina gave a short, sharp laugh, and shook her head. "I don't know why. What did you do in Casiti?"

"I was a student, and a doctor."

"A doctor?" She looked very surprised. "You can treat sick people?"

"Yes, I can. I'm looking for a hospital to work in."

She laughed again. "Ain't no hospital will hire you. But I know a lot of people who need doctoring. My nephew is real sick—he probably will die. We haven't been able to get no one to see him. Will you see him?"

"Of course. Where is he?"

"Finish your soup, and I'll take you to him."

Jam'elo hurriedly finished his soup, and then he followed Dina out of her house, and down the street to a house that looked well-kept, like Dina's. She knocked at the door.

"Ada! I got a doctor here to look at James!"

The door was opened by a haggard looking woman with a skin tone similar to Dina's.

"A docta? Where'd you fine a docta?"

"Ada, this here is Jameelo. He's traveling, and he says he can help."

Jam'elo nodded. "Yes, I can help. Can I see him?"

Ada said, shaking her head, "He too far gone, he gonna die soon. But if you wanna try, who am I to stop it? Follow me."

Ada walked into the house, and Jam'elo and Dina followed. It was dark, and it took Jam'elo a little time to get used to the dimness. In a room in the back lay a small boy. Jam'elo thought he was probably around eight or nine Earth years old.

Jam'elo examined the boy. He was feverish and clearly had trouble breathing. His glands were swollen, and when he opened the boy's mouth, he saw a thick, gray coating in his throat and on his tonsils. He suspected agent 24. He swabbed the throat, and surreptitiously used his diagnostic instrument. Yes, agent 24 it was. He took out a small bottle from his kit with the broad-spectrum antibiotic that would take care of diseases brought on by agents in the class of 24.

"Can you boil some water, please?" He didn't want to compound the troubles of agent 24 with agent 31, which he had learned was often found in the water in communities like this.

Ada left the room, and after a while came back with cup full of hot water.

"Thank you."

Jam'elo waited a little while for the water to cool, then put a few drops of his antibiotic in the water. He propped up the boy's head.

"You need to drink a little of this now."

The boy nodded and drank some of the liquid.

Jam'elo turned to Ada. "He needs to finish this cup of water over the next few hours. His symptoms should diminish, and he should be somewhat better by morning. It will take him a few days to completely recover."

"That all?"

"Yes, that's it."

Ada shook her head sadly, and said, "I don't see how that gonna hep him..."

Jam'elo took Ada's hands in his and looked in her eyes.

"Ada, I know you don't know me, and have no reason to trust me. But your son will be fine."

In truth, the boy had already taken in enough of the antibiotic to cure agent 24, albeit more slowly than it could, because he had diluted it so much. The antibiotics, nanoparticles impossible for anyone on Earth to detect, could deal with foreign infections found here almost immediately with one dose. But he knew from his studies that the medicine at this time could not work that way, and it would be deemed too miraculous if the boy recovered too quickly with only one dose.

"I'll come back to check on him in the morning. If for some reason he takes a turn for the worse, please come get me at the Chissler's dwelling."

Ada nodded and sat next to her son. Jam'elo and Dina left to return back to her house.

Baton Rouge, Louisiana, April 15, 1859

Emma knew what was going on upstairs. She looked up at the tall ceiling, as if to peer into the rooms above and find out exactly what was happening. Her master was dying. He might already be dead. He had gotten sick almost six months ago, and she had seen this doctor and that doctor visit. No one would tell her exactly what was wrong with him.

She knew that her fate, and the fate of all on the plantation, was in the hands of her master's son. She had never liked him much; she thought he was mean for no good reason. And last month, when he'd caught her teaching her daughter how to read, he had punished her badly. She knew that he would rather be out West, and like a lot of the slaves, she expected that one of his first deeds would be to sell them all, along with the plantation.

But such thinking was useless when she had so much to do. She had to help Ginny get the roast done, shell the peas, and make the table, all in the next hour. Even though her master was on his deathbed, his family went on as if nothing was happening—they were entertaining again tonight.

She walked into the kitchen, to see a large bowl with pea pods on the table.

"Emma, where you been? Those peas ain't gonna shell themselves, girl." Emma looked at Ginny, the portly woman who ran the kitchen for their master.

"Sorry Ginny, I been running errands young Massa done give me. I'm here now."

Emma sat down at the table, and started to shell the peas, as Ginny bustled about in the kitchen preparing other food for dinner.

"So, Ginny, what do you think gonna happen to us?"

"There ain't no reason to spend energy tryin' ta figure it out, girl. What will happen, will happen. Young Massa don' want to be here, and don' want us, so I 'spect we're all gonna be sold. But there ain't no reason to cry none. Any other Massa gonna just be the same."

"Why Massa dying? What ya think is wrong wit' 'im?"

"Emma, why you wanna know that? You always asking those kinda questions. Stop now, and shell those peas, girl!"

She stopped talking, but the worrying and wondering didn't stop any. She shelled the peas, and then assisted Ginny with preparing the table. She still couldn't get her mind off of the future.

She heard the guests arrive in the dining room, and her master's son regaling them with his travel tales. He had been out West for a while and had only come back last year when his father took ill. She knew he liked to think of himself as a rugged individualist and a mountain man.

She walked into the dining room, carrying a large tray with rolls for the table. She ignored the discussion around her, until it became clear that the master's son was talking about her. She had learned the fine art of listening while pretending not to be present when she was spoken of in the third person by her masters.

"See Emma, here. She is quite beautiful, isn't she? I imagine she'll fetch me a great price. Did you know she used to be at the Langston plantation? Turns out John there had a bit of a thing for her, and he got her pregnant. When John's wife found out, she forced him to sell her. I got a great deal on her and her git. I expect I'll do better if I sell them separately—Martin Huber has already shown interest in the daughter."

Emma's emotions threatened to overwhelm her. She got out of the dining room as soon as it was possible, and ran through the kitchen outside, where she threw up what was in her stomach. She vaguely heard Ginny next to her comforting her, then telling her to get inside to finish helping bring the food out. She couldn't bear it and ran out into the night.

A few days later, after her master died, she was coming back to her room after a long day of work. Her daughter was sitting in the room, reading a primer, and looked up to see her, with a worried look on her face.

"Mama, where you been?"

"Baby, I've been busy. Now that Massa is dead, Missus and young Massa give me a lot to do. I'm sorry I haven't been around much. Auntie Nellie says you been behaving well."

"I like Auntie Nellie, Mama, but I miss seeing you."

"Baby, I'm here. Don' worry."

Emma and her daughter May were sitting in their small room, underneath the west wing of the large plantation house. The room could be cold, and the unusually biting weather this week meant that they were huddled together with blankets. Emma had started a fire in the small fireplace which took off some of the chill in the room, but never made it truly warm.

Emma had spent the day helping see to the arrangements for the guests that were arriving at the plantation for the funeral. She had been back and forth between the mistress' rooms and other parts of the house all day, preparing guest rooms, doing laundry, and helping Ginny with the menu planning.

She tucked May into her bed and waited until she was asleep. Then she opened the book that she had taken surreptitiously from her master's library several months ago. Now that her master was dead, he wouldn't miss the book, and she knew that neither his son, nor his wife would care about it. The book was her prized possession, now; it was called "Outlines of Astronomy."

She remembered when she was a child, she always wondered about what was in the sky. The stars, the moon, and the sun all intrigued her, and she asked everyone she could find about them. Most people either ignored her questions or gave her answers like "God and the angels are in the sky." That was never satisfying to her. She knew there was much more to it than that.

Her old master John would answer her questions and tell her about the constellations and planets in the sky. He used to spend time outside with something he called a "telescope." He even allowed her to look through it at the moon, once. He said that the study of the night sky was called "Astronomy." She remembered that word, and one day, when she was doing errands for her current master, she saw the book on the shelf with that word in the title; she knew she wanted that book. Finally, she was able to grab it, and she had been trying to read it ever since. It was slow going—she didn't understand a lot of the words that it used, but she kept at it, and she was learning a little bit at a time. After a while of reading, her eyes and her head got tired. It was time for sleep. She put out the lamp.

As she lay there in the dark, her mind went back over the day. She had overheard the missus and young Massa talking—the missus was going to move north to Connecticut to be with her sister, and they were going to sell all of the slaves and the plantation by the beginning of summer, when young Massa planned to leave to go back West. Her fate was sealed. She just hoped that she and her daughter could remain together. She planned to ask young Massa about it.

She thought about how she would ask him, and she imagined him being noble, and gentle, and letting them stay together. As she drifted to sleep, a voice warned her not to be too hopeful, not to expect too much. She slept fitfully and dreamed dreams of separation and loss.

Saint Paul, Minnesota, 118 Paqn, 742/April 15, 1859

Jam'elo, Lou and Dina were sitting around the kitchen table. Jam'elo had just come back from a completely unsuccessful day of trying to find a place in a local hospital to work as a doctor. He was explaining his experience to Lou and Dina over dinner.

"I just don't understand it. Never did they ask me any questions to figure out whether or not I knew medicine. Never did they have me work with someone who needed help. They just took one look at me and asked me to leave. One hospital had a sign looking for doctors, but it didn't matter."

Dina said, "Jameelo, din't I tell you nobody hire you?"

Jam'elo nodded. "You did, Dina. I'm sorry I didn't believe you. I have a question for you. One man who I talked to called me a 'mulatto'. What is that?"

Lou snorted, and Dina shook her head. "Jameelo, a mulatto is a mix between a white and a negro. Mostly, those slave-owners in the South get their slaves pregnant. Those chillen' are mulatto, or quadroon – they a mix. It don't matter how little negro blood you got, you know. Even just a little is enough."

Jam'elo refrained from explaining his own origin, and the fact that he certainly did have a little negro blood. And, of course, he had a little of everything else.

They heard a knock at the door, and Gregory, Lou's brother, and the father of James, the child that Jam'elo treated, walked into the house.

"Jameelo, James got up this afternoon, and he done walked around! He's doing much better. I don't know how to thank you—we were sure he was gonna die."

"I'm glad I could help. I'll check in on him again tomorrow, and make sure he's recovering properly."

"Greg, come over here and get some food. There are some greens on the stove, and the corn bread just came out of the oven."

"Ooh, that's my favorite!"

The four of them sat at the table, with Lou, Gregory and Dina talking amiably about their family and the goings on in the community. Jam'elo was listening and observing. They didn't seem to mind that he didn't participate in their conversation. At one point, the topic changed dramatically.

Gregory asked, "Did'ja meet dat man Joseph, dat just arrived? He Jason's cousin."

Lou answered, "I sure heard about him. He's de talk of de town. He'd better be careful, some bounty hunter gonna fine out about him."

"He done made it all the way up from South Carolina. Brave fellow. I heard he almost got killed three or four times on de way."

Lou laughed. "I dunno - I think he's trying to make some kinda name for hisself."

"But you got to give him credit—escaping Carolina ain't easy."

Jam'elo figured that he'd gotten to know these people well enough to take the risk of asking a question.

He asked, "Are many people able to escape from slavery in the South?"

Dina looked at him with deep suspicion. Lou shook his head. "Jameelo, how is it you don't know nothin'?"

"I'm sorry, I meant no offense. I've only been in this country for a short time. There is a lot I don't know."

Dina asked, "Does everyone where you come from look like you?"

Jam'elo nodded. "Pretty much."

"Do you have slavery?"

"No. We were slaves, a long time ago."

"You escaped?"

"We were freed."

Lou cut in. "Dina, why you asking the man all those questions? Jam'elo, we hope that all Negroes will be freed soon."

Dina laughed. "Lou, you a silly man sometimes. Ain't no one gonna free anyone down South. We can be free up here, but no one really cares enough to free anyone down there. My mother was lucky to make it out before now—these days, she'd likely be caught and sent back. Glad I was born free up here."

They talked for a while about the goings on in the country, then Gregory said, "My boss is goin' ta Oregon in a few weeks. I'm gonna need to fine me a new job."

Jam'elo asked, "Why is he going?"

"He's leading a bunch of people out there to farm and that kind of thing."

Jam'elo wondered whether it might be a good idea for him to try and join this group. He wanted to travel, and this might be a good way to do that. Gregory could vouch for him.

"Do you think he might want a doctor along?"

Gregory shrugged his shoulders. "I don' know, but I'll ask 'im."

Saint Paul, Minnesota, 124 Paqn, 742/April 30, 1859

Jam'elo was sitting at the kitchen table, reading the newspaper, and looked up as he heard the door knock. Gregory walked in.

"Hey Jameelo—I talked wit' my boss. He like to meet you and see if he wanna take you on the trip to Oregon. Apparently there ain't no doctors who want to go wit' him."

"Where can I find him?"

"I'll take you to him. We can go now if you wanna."

Jam'elo got up, and followed Gregory out of the house, and down several streets, to the wharves. They went into one of the large warehouse buildings near the ships.

"Mr. Thomas, dis here is Jameelo, the doctor that done cured my son."

A tall man stepped forward. He had a beard and was wearing formal attire: what Jameelo had learned was frock coat over a waist coat. After the first few days here, Jam'elo had wondered whether it had been his much less formal attire that had been part of the problem, but after he was able to obtain his own set of more formal clothing, no one's behavior had changed much, so he went back to his old clothing that was at least more comfortable.

"Hello Jameelo. What's your last name?"

"Kadarin."

"Kadarin? You have a strange name."

"I'm from far away."

"So, you are a doctor?"

"Yes. I will be happy to serve your company's medical needs during the trip to Oregon."

"Where did you go to school to become a doctor?"

"In my home, Casiti."

"I hear you cured some bad infections, and birthed a couple of babies?"

Jam'elo nodded. "Yes, all are doing well."

"I can't pay you all that much—I can feed you, provide you with a horse, and give you about two dollars a month."

"That would be sufficient; I don't need much."

Mr. Thomas looked at Jam'elo and narrowed his eyes, then Jam'elo could see his face relax.

"Well, Gregory here trusts you, and I trust him, so I'll take you on. We leave in four days: first thing in the morning. We're taking a steamboat to meet most of our group in Davenport. Meet us here, and we'll make our way to the Steamship docks."

Jam'elo had learned the custom of shaking hands, and he stuck out his hand to Mr. Thomas. They shook hands.

"Thank you very much. I'll be here."

As Gregory and Jam'elo walked back to the Chissler's, Jam'elo asked, "Are you going out to Oregon?"

Gregory shook his head.

"I wanted to, but Oregon don't allow no negroes, and I'd risk it, but my wife... she scared for our kids. I understand."

Jam'elo let that settle in his mind. He couldn't really make himself understand it.

Chapter 2

Expedition Log 742.4.4 Student: Jam'elo z Kadarin. Date: 127 Paqn 742

I have attached myself to a group of settlers heading toward Oregon. Mr. Thomas is the leader of that group, and he is bringing five families from Saint Paul, and meeting about twenty other families in Davenport, Iowa, to start on the Oregon Trail. We will end up in Oregon City, Oregon. Mr. Thomas has been quite friendly to me, which is a departure from the behavior of many individuals with lighter skin tone here in Saint Paul.

We leave in a few days on a steamship, called "The Metropolitan." I look forward to experiencing this form of travel on Reit'al, and meeting those who also find themselves on the river.

I have sent commands to my AI to set listening devices along our route, so there should be quite a bit of climate and activity data. The whole trip will take approximately 150 Reit'al days. We'll arrive in the fall. I hope that I'll be able to find my place in Oregon to gather more information.

I will be a little sorry to leave this community so soon, but it seems important for me to see as much as possible of this continent during this expedition to understand more about the social structures and dynamics here at this time.

Outside Canemah, Oregon, April–May 1859

Robert's voice boomed from the front of the cabin, "I'm going into town, and I expect a good dinner when I get back."

Lena then heard him more quietly say to their daughter Clara, "Father will be home straight away, and I will bring you a nice gift. You've been a very good girl this week."

Lena sometimes had a hard time with the differences between the way her husband treated her, and the way he treated their children. She didn't resent it, really—she was happy that he showed them love. But he never showed her any love, and basically had treated her as he would treat a slave these past seven years of marriage. After they had first married, when they were taking a trip to Paris for their honeymoon, he was different. Then he was charming and gracious; not loving, quite, but at least pleasant. That had worn off on the trip west to Oregon and disappeared once they had settled into life on their ranch. She doubted he even liked her. She certainly didn't like him very much.

As she was cleaning up their bedroom, she found one of his handkerchiefs on the floor under the bed. She wished he were a little neater. When she picked up the handkerchief, she noticed large spots of blood. He had been coughing a lot lately, and feeling unwell, and she wondered whether the blood was related. She would have suggested that he go to the doctor, except the only doctor had left town for California last week.

Two weeks later, Lena sat in the front room of their cabin, mending some shirts. Robert had become so ill that he was bedridden. He would die soon, that much was certain.

"Bring me that opium syrup! I'm in pain!" Lena could hear her husband's agitated voice from the front room of their cabin. She got up, picked up the sweet, sticky syrup, and went into the bedroom to give it to him. The room smelled terrible, since he'd been in bed for so many days, unable to get up. Lena knew it was time for her to clean him up again.

"Here you are, Robert. You'll feel better soon."

She gave him the syrup, and after he harangued her for a while, he finally fell into a stupor. She used that stupor to her advantage, and cleaned him up, and moved him around so she could put new sheets on the bed.

They hadn't had benefit of a doctor for a few weeks since the only doctor in town left to move to California. Her husband had been rapidly deteriorating, and the end was coming near. She'd had a conversation with her daughter Clara, who was old enough to understand what death meant, and Clara would miss her father. Robert Jr. was only two years old and didn't really even know his father.

She gathered up all of the soiled bedclothes and other items and brought them outside and put them in the large barrel she had been using for the laundry. She went back inside to stoke the fire in the stove to heat up some hot water that she'd use to soak the linens in. As she went about the laundry and other tasks, she couldn't help but reflect on how she'd gotten to this place.

She had never done her own laundry until she and Robert packed up and left Richmond to find their fortunes out West. She had been happy to find a way out of Richmond—that was the only reason she married Robert. All of her other prospects were men who were in line to take over their family plantations, or were part of Richmond society, and planned to stay, and she wanted no part of it. She hated Virginia, and everything about it, and was happy to be gone as soon as she could.

Robert had been worse than she originally thought. He had some charm, for sure, but he saved that for strangers, and their children. He was smart, but often angry, and almost always mean. He was the youngest son of a very prominent family and had been spoiled; he was very difficult to live with.

She felt mixed feelings about the fact that he would die soon, although none of them included sadness. She'd have to manage on her own without him, and she didn't know what that would be like out here in Oregon. She didn't much like most men and attaching herself to any of the single or widowed men she'd met so far was out of the question. She would be happy to no longer have to endure Robert's critical comments, his mean temper, or his rough, fumbling attention in their bed. Moving back to Virginia was the very last thing she wanted. She would have to make do here.

She finally finished the long list of chores, fed and put her children to bed, and checked on Robert, who was still asleep. She sat in front of the fireplace reading one of the books she'd picked up in Paris but hadn't had a chance to read yet. It was called "Adolphe." She lost herself in the pages of French romance for a while, and then fell asleep.

She felt a tug at her hand, which woke her up.

"Mama, Papa is cold." Lena shook herself awake to see her daughter looking at her with a strange look on her face. Cold?

"Is that what he told you, sweetheart?" Clara shook her head.

"No, Mama, he is still asleep. I tried to wake him up, and when I touched him, his hand was cold."

Lena knew that Robert must have died overnight.

"I'll see what's going on, sweetheart. Stay here, alright?" Clara nodded, and Lena went back to the bedroom that she usually shared with her husband. She stood over him and could see the film beginning to form over his eyes. He was definitely dead. She felt a wave of relief, and she began to sob.

After a little bit, she heard next to her, "Is he dead, mama?"

She turned to Clara. "Yes, Clara, he's dead. Please go get your brother and help him get dressed. I need to go into town and get someone to help us with your father's body."

Two days later, Lena looked around at the small group of people gathered around Robert's grave. They were in the cemetery of the small Methodist Church of Canemah. The grass had returned to being green, and there would be some flowers for Robert's grave. Her feelings upon his death were as conflicted as they had been while he was sick. She was both relieved and scared.

"Unto Almighty God we commend the soul of our brother departed, and we commit his body to the ground; earth to earth, ashes to ashes, dust to dust."

The words of the minister droned on, and she was hardly paying attention. Her daughter Clara stirred by her side, and she looked down, and put her hand gently on Clara's shoulder. Clara looked up at her, and Lena smiled, trying to express to Clara that it would all be alright.

"...according to the mighty working whereby He is able to subdue all things unto Himself."

The minister paused, then looked up at the group gathered, and said "The Lord be with you."

Lena managed to croak with everyone, "And with thy spirit."

It was over. The group broke up, and Lena walked with Clara out of the cemetery to their wagon. A neighbor friend had agreed to watch Robert Jr. during the funeral, and Lena wanted to get back to the house, and finally start her new life. She had so much to do. She had managed to clean up the house once Robert's body was taken out. But she had a long list of things that hadn't gotten accomplished during his illness, including preparing her garden.

As she reached her wagon, a slight man with a graying beard walked up to her, and said, "Mrs. Jameson?"

She remembered him as the post office manager. She inclined her head slightly and dipped into an almost imperceptible curtsy. She wasn't all that interested in engaging in conversation.

"Hello Mr. Klyde."

"I'm sorry for your loss, Mrs. Jameson. I know life as a widow is difficult out here. I expect you'll be returning to Virginia soon."

"You would be mistaken, Mr. Klyde. I'm staying on the ranch."

"I see. Well, if there is anything I can do to help, please let me know."

She smiled, knowing that he was a widower, and probably hoping to be in line as a suitor.

"Thank you so much, Mr. Klyde. I'll keep that in mind."

"Please call me Joseph."

She said, "Excuse me, Mr. Klyde, I must get back to my homestead."

She could tell he looked crestfallen. He stepped away from the wagon, and she picked Clara up and put her inside, then climbed up herself, and snapped the reigns. She realized that she would have to remain on extremely formal terms with men from this time forward.

The days and weeks after Robert's funeral were hectic yet satisfying. She felt good about arranging the cabin and the ranch to suit herself, instead of Robert. She spent many an evening reading instead of having to listen to Robert rant on about this or that issue. She was able to spend more time with Clara and Robert Jr. now that she wasn't at Robert's beck and call.

The day after Independence Day, Lena had some errands in town she needed to attend to, so she hitched up the wagon, put Clara and Robert Jr. in it, and rode into town. The banners and flags were still up, but the town was quiet. It seemed a normal Tuesday in the small town. She had chosen to avoid the celebrations in town yesterday; today she needed to get the post, pick up a few supplies, and drop off her vegetables at the store.

Lena had been able to make ends meet so far. She had some leftover money from her husband's estate—money he had been given by his father for the trip West. She had her garden growing, and it had become productive. She'd had the foresight a few years ago to plant a large fruit orchard, and that was coming in handy. She imagined that her apple harvest might make a difference this fall. She expected that she would be able to sell enough vegetables and fruits to pay for much of the flour, grain, cloth and other supplies she and her children needed. She wasn't sure what would happen during the winter, although she had been also selling some of her surplus preserves.

After going to the store to sell her vegetables and pick up her supplies, she walked into the post office to see Mr. Klyde behind the desk. By now, he had figured out that she wasn't interested in him, or any man, and had left her alone.

"Hello Mrs. Jameson. How are you today?" His tone was formal.

"I'm fine, thank you, Mr. Klyde."

"I have a letter for you, from Virginia. Also, I have a small package addressed to Mr. Jameson."

"I'll take them, thank you."

When she was at home, and had put Robert Jr. and Clara to bed, she sat next to her fireplace, and opened the letter from her mother. Her mother expressed her condolences again. This was at least the fifth letter she had received from her mother since she sent word of Robert's death. She spent the rest of the letter explaining why Lena should return to Richmond, to the plantation. Her mother told the news of the plantation, such as an increase in the number of slaves, the large tobacco harvests, some new foremen, her brother's involvement in Virginia politics, and other things that Lena really had no interest in.

Her mother would not understand her insistence on staying here in Oregon, nor her preference for the life that she was making here. No, there wasn't anyone to cook her food, or raise her children, or grow her vegetables, but she was happy doing all of that independently. And she was happy that she would never live in that environment again. She didn't want to raise her children to treat some people differently than others.

She decided it was time to look at the package addressed to Robert. The package had a return address of London, England, with British postage. She opened it up, and carefully unwrapped the paper, and then cloth surrounding the object inside. It was a pocket watch, with a quite beautiful engraving on the front of the cover. Lena knew that Robert had paid quite a sum for that watch. She chuckled at the thought that he never got it. She didn't know what she would do with it.

Baton Rouge, Louisiana, June 1869

"But Massa, she needs me!"

Emma looked at her master's son, who was tall, had reddish hair, and a stern face.

"Emma, your daughter is already spoken for—and the buyer doesn't want you. I'm sorry. She'll be fine with Mr. Huber."

"But he'll put her in da fields, Massa! She no field hand."

He put his hand over her upper arm, hurting her. She realized that she'd crossed a line. But she'd been desperate.

"Emma, go away. We have no more to talk about."

He let go, and she slowly turned, and walked toward the door of the living room.

"And bring me a hot toddy, please. I'm not feeling so well."

She left to go to the kitchen and prepare his drink. She prepared it quickly and brought it to him. He was busy reading the newspaper, so she set it down next to him. He didn't even look up. She left and went downstairs to the room she shared with her daughter. Her daughter was there reading the primer Emma had managed to steal without anyone noticing.

"Mama! I'm almost finished with this book!"

"That's great, baby." She broke down and started to cry. She couldn't help the feelings welling up inside of her, threatening to break her apart.

"Mama, what's wrong?"

After a while, she gained control of herself.

"It's OK, baby, don't worry." She wiped her eyes and her nose and helped May read the rest of the primer. She wished she knew of a way to leave and take her daughter far away from this place.

A week or so later, she was working in the kitchen, when Ginny came in.

"That Mister Huber jus' got 'ere."

"What?"

"I don't know what he here for—maybe to pick up the slaves he bought."

"May! He come to get May!"

Emma ran out of the kitchen, leaving the food she was cooking, and went outside looking around. She saw her master talking to Mr. Huber.

"Mamma!"

She turned around to see Cole, one of the foremen, with her hands around May's upper arm, pulling her toward Mr. Huber's wagon.

Emma ran toward May, and tried to hug her, and take her away from Cole, but he got in between them, and before she knew it, she felt rough hands on her, dragging her away from May. She knew it was her master. She turned to see his face, which was suffused with red.

"Emma, I told you that your daughter was to be sold. Behave, now, or I'll send you to Cole for the lash."

"Massa, please! She's all I got!"

She felt a hand across her cheek, and she tasted blood and fell to the ground. She looked up to see May being put into the wagon.

"Mama, Mama!"

She watched as the wagon rolled away, and her daughter looked at her with tears streaming down her face, and the most distraught look Emma had ever seen. All that Emma could do was sit on the dusty ground of the driveway and sob.

A week later, Emma was standing on a platform, and all eyes were on her. The slaves that hadn't yet been sold were rousted out of bed early that morning, put in chains, and driven in a wagon to the auction house. She looked around the large room. There was a small group of slaves from her plantation remaining—she was in the last group. She looked toward the large audience of men, some looking with disinterest, some with the interest of a potential buyer, and others looking at her in a way that made her feel vulnerable and ashamed.

"Here we have a healthy female, aged about twenty-five, no illness, no disease. She's already a proven child bearer. She has worked as a house nigger, and we are told she is a good cook. She can take care of children as well. We are beginning this auction at nine hundred dollars."

Emma let the sounds from the auction wash over her. When her daughter had been taken, something inside her had closed up, and she felt like it would never open again. She had never asked to bear her daughter, but she loved her daughter more than life. She didn't care what happened next.

She thought about that moment nine years ago. She had been minding her own business, doing the final cleaning of the kitchen for the night, when her master John came in, smelling of whiskey. He had apologized for insulting her during dinner. He was being nice—she appreciated it. Then he started to kiss and caress her, and she felt conflicted. She didn't know what to do. She knew she couldn't fight him off —she'd be punished. And he seemed sweet at that moment—perhaps a man she could almost like. His attention felt good to her then. After a little while, he lifted her skirts, and dropped his pants. It had been quick, and not unpleasant.

Afterwards, he was always nice to her—never insulting or cruel, as he sometimes would be to others. Once she started showing, his wife became suspicious, and eventually confronted her. She had no choice but to tell her what had happened. The next thing she knew, she was sold to Master Kildare. And now she was here and would soon be in the hands of another master. And her daughter was gone.

Finally, the auction was over. A plump older man in the far corner had bought her. She stepped down from the platform and was taken toward her new master.

Mississippi River, 128 Paqn, 742/May 7, 1859

Jam'elo stood on the edge of the deck, leaning on the railing that was taller than his waist. He looked out over the expanse of the river, examining what he could see on the banks. Sometimes there were tall trees on one or both sides of the river. Other times, there would be farmland, where Jam'elo could see dwellings and animals. They had been on the river for a day and would be arriving at their final destination tomorrow. He was soothed by the water, and the slow pace of travel on the river. He had been enchanted by its size. It was larger than any river on Casiti.

The weather had finally cleared after a horrible thunderstorm, and lightening had struck the ship, creating some chaos on board. Finally, though, things had settled down, and no one was injured, so Jam'elo's skills hadn't been needed.

He had been the object of some amount of curiosity, and a few times outright hostility from some of the passengers of the steamboat. Jam'elo felt like he no longer really paid much attention to the reactions of those around him. On the other hand, he kept to himself more and more, and tried to avoid as many interactions with strangers as he could, so he knew that he was still affected by their responses to him.

He was happy to be traveling, and he was looking forward to seeing the country that they would be going through. He'd seen some satellite and holographic imaging of the mountains, so he knew that crossing over them would be a very different experience.

"It's quite a beautiful river, isn't it?" Jam'elo turned to see Curtis walking up to the railing and looking out.

Jam'elo said, "Yes, it is, indeed."

"Do you have any rivers like this where you come from?"

"Not like this, no. We have rivers, but none that get this wide or deep. We can't travel on them."

Curtis was Mr. Thomas' son, a young man of 18 who had befriended Jam'elo. Curtis seemed to like him, and Jam'elo had decided to make Curtis his assistant. He knew he could teach Curtis a lot of the simpler treatments—treatments he could do without any Casitian technology.

"I'm looking forward to finally getting on the road. My father gave me a huge list of things I need to help him obtain when we get to Davenport."

"If you want some help, I'd be glad to assist. I don't have much to do until we get on the road."

Curtis smiled and nodded.

"That would be great! Thanks. Just make sure you tell father you volunteered."

They talked for a while amiably about the journey, and what it might be like. Curtis knew less than Jam'elo did about what the terrain ahead would bring.

They heard the bell for dinner and went inside to the large dining hall. Jam'elo was surprised by the complaints that others on the boat had of the food during the journey. Jam'elo had uniformly liked all of the food since he landed on Earth, including the food here. Before he could sit down, Mr. Thomas came up to him.

"Jameelo, one of our company took sick last night. She thought that it would pass, but it has not. After dinner, can you look in on her? It's Mrs. Knowlton."

"Certainly, Mr. Thomas, I'll be glad to," Jam'elo replied.

Dinner passed in a blur, except for an especially heated conversation between two men who were not in their company about the rights of citizens to own slaves. Jam'elo turned on the recording device he kept in his pocket. He would ask his AI to transcribe the argument later.

He walked to the Knowlton's cabin and knocked on the door. Mr. Knowlton answered it.

"Ah, Jameelo. I'm glad you are here. Please come in. Mrs. Knowlton is quite ill."

Jam'elo entered the room and stood next to the bed where Mrs. Knowlton was lying. He could see she was feverish, with clammy skin. She appeared to be asleep or unconscious.

"When did this start?"

"Late last night. She was sick—she lost her dinner, and also had terrible diarrhea."

Jam'elo thought that it was likely agent 45, a common kind of bacterium found in spoiled food. He took out a cotton swab and swabbed inside her mouth briefly. Then he surreptitiously placed the swab inside his small diagnostic device. Yes, agent 45 it was. He took out his broad-spectrum antibacterial treatment, disguised as a kind of tincture.

"I'm going to give her this tincture. Please make sure she drinks a lot of water. She should be better by the time we need to leave the boat tomorrow."

He gently woke her up and asked her to swallow the spoonful of liquid. She did. He then gave her a cup of water to drink. He left them, knowing that she would be fine in the morning.

He went in search for Mr. Thomas. If one person had been infected with agent 45, it was likely there would be others. He thought it might be a busy night.

Outside Davenport Iowa, 133 Paqn, 742/May 15, 1859

Jam'elo rode his horse alongside the wagon train. He felt a little unsure on his horse, even though he had gotten some practice before they had left Saint Paul. There were 30 wagons in the train, and about one hundred men, women and children in this company. Jam'elo had met most of them, and in general, they had been friendly and welcoming to him.

In meeting all of the party, Jam'elo was struck by how varied the groups were. It was largely families, although there were a few unattached single men, like Jam'elo. They were mostly young families, and many had saved everything they had to make this journey. Some had even immigrated directly from countries across the ocean. They all had hopes of creating new lives and making success where they had failed before.

They had left Davenport just after dawn and had several days of travel ahead within relatively populated areas. People would mostly be staying in their wagons at night. Jam'elo, like some others, would be sleeping out in the open. The nights were still a bit chilly at times, but for Jam'elo, it was fairly warm compared to what he was used to on Casiti.

Jam'elo looked behind him at the long row of wagons, most with billowing white covers, a few without. He was following the small group of men at the front. He was toward the back of that group, just ahead of the Thomas wagon.

He could already tell it was going to be a long and busy trip for him. First, there was the outbreak of agent 45 on the steamship. Then, in Davenport, he'd heard all sorts of stories about people going West getting sick, getting attacked and robbed by "Indians" and other types of physical dangers. Most of what he carried was on his horse with him, but he had a small amount of medical supplies in the wagon with the Thomas family belongings. Mr. Thomas and Curtis rode horses, but Curtis' younger siblings, Joseph, who was 10, and Maybelle, who was 8, rode in the wagon that was driven by Mrs. Thomas.

Jam'elo knew about the people they called the "Indians." Some people used different names for them and some referred to them by tribal names. Jam'elo had read everything he could about the fated expedition to this continent in 702. The Casitians had met and were spending time with a local indigenous people in the southeast of the continent, when a group of settlers mounted a surprise attack on the village they were staying in. One Casitian was gravely wounded, and that had ended the expedition. It was the first time in many years that a Casitian had been in physical danger during an expedition to Earth. They had learned from their listening devices later that the indigenous people had retaliated by mounting their own attack on the settlers. Jam'elo wondered what the historians of this day had to say about that incident.

Jam'elo had started reading the newspaper in Saint Paul, and he'd picked up a Davenport Daily Gazette from a few days ago to read at his leisure on the trip. He knew he could get a few more newspapers on the way in the next few weeks, but after they headed into Nebraska territory, points of civilization were going to be few and far between.

Reading the newspaper helped him understand more of what was going on: the political process, the details of people's everyday lives, and the stress of a country he could tell was straining apart.

He turned his attention back to the wagon train, as he heard a horse draw close to his side.

He said, "That's quite the wagon train, eh?"

Jam'elo looked to his left to see Curtis on his horse. He smiled.

"Yes, it is. I've never seen anything like it."

"Neither have I! I heard stories from one of the suppliers that just ahead of us was a wagon train with more than 100 families!"

"I guess we might catch up to them—your father seems bent on speed."

"He'd like to make it in less than 150 days—that's the standard time it takes. But I'm not sure that this group is up to such a fast pace."

They rode in companionable silence for a long while. Up ahead, Jam'elo could see Mr. Thomas coming back their way. When he arrived, he sidled his horse next to his son's.

"Curtis, can you please go back to the end of the train and check on Jason and John who are supposed to be keeping the cattle together? On the last hill we crested, I looked back to see the cattle scattered all over the place."

"Sure thing, father." Curtis moved outside of the line, turned around, and put his horse into a gallop headed toward the back.

"So, Jameelo, what do you think of this?"

"It is certainly a massive undertaking, Mr. Thomas. I hope that we have a smooth journey. I know it's going to be a long one."

"There aren't a lot of people traveling this way between here and Grand Island. We'll have a nice stop in Nebraska City—we can get resupplied there. Once we get onto the main course of the trail, we won't be alone much—and the less we're alone, the safer we are. The other part I worry about is getting over the mountains."

"Mr. Thomas, it seems like we've got a pretty hardy bunch."

He chuckled, then seemed thoughtful.

"I hope so. I'm surely glad we have you around."

Jam'elo said, "I've no doubt my services will be required."

Oregon Trail, 25 Musb, 742/July 1, 1859

Jam'elo kicked the stirrups to encourage his horse to keep walking to the top of the small hillock. He stopped, turned his horse, and looked down to see the rest of the wagon train and Independence Rock in the distance behind them. They had reached that landmark ahead of schedule, so they had decided to rest for a few days in the company of another group of travelers. Jam'elo had been very busy treating both parties for various ailments and injuries, but he had gotten some rest in the last day.

He was excited to keep going. It had been a largely uneventful trip so far, with a few interactions with Indians, and some altercations between members of their party. There had been an especially tough few days when there had been a storm that had mired their party in mud. He felt like he was finally hitting his stride: being able to tell which people he could trust, and be comfortable with, and which people didn't like him just because of how he looked.

He was learning a lot about why people were traveling West, and what they hoped to accomplish. Some just wanted land for their families, so that they could farm and raise animals, some hoped to start businesses, and others wanted to find gold.

Most of it was hard for him to fathom. His society was one that had been established long ago and had gone through very little change in more than 2500 Earth years. Earth had been in a much more primitive state at the beginning of his own culture than it was now. For him, it felt like a gift to be present in a time of such turmoil and change, and to get to witness so much of it personally.

He heard the clop of hooves approaching and saw Curtis on his horse cantering toward him. He waved and slowed down.

"Hello Curtis. How has the day been for you so far? I haven't seen much of you."

"My father gave me the job of making sure that all of the cattle were accounted for and in place. He also wanted me to check on some families to make sure that they weren't straggling too much."

"Ah, that sounds like it would keep you busy. I've finally gotten some rest from all of the doctoring I've been doing lately."

"Yes, you've been quite busy yourself, haven't you?" Curtis chuckled, and continued, "I know that you've been giving Mrs. Matthew quite a bit of attention. If she wasn't already married, I'd think she'd fallen for you."

Jam'elo smiled and nodded. He had noticed that women did seem to like him, and that he too often had to fend off the attention of the few unmarried women in the party.

He and Curtis rode on for a while. He had a few burning questions, and Curtis always seemed willing to entertain Jam'elo's curiosity.

"Curtis, yesterday we had an interaction with some Indians, the Pawnee, you said."

"Yeah. Since we outnumbered them, they were just going to make nice."

"They offered us some things."

Curtis laughed. "I noticed you bought some beads."

"They looked interesting."

"They are worthless."

"Worthless? They were very nicely made—artistic."

Curtis laughed. "I noticed how they looked at you. They think you are one of them, maybe?"

Jam'elo shook his head. "I think I just looked unusual to them. They know I'm not one of them."

"You're not one of anybody are you?"

Jam'elo smiled at Curtis and said, "I guess that's about as close as you can get to the truth. Curtis, why don't you like them?"

He curled his lip. "They are uncivilized, dirty, violent..."

"Violent?"

"Yes, they will attack at almost any provocation."

"But Curtis, people are taking the land they have lived on for a long time and forcing them off."

"They don't deserve it. We can do better with it."

Jam'elo was silent. He was surprised at Curtis's attitude. He didn't quite know what to say, or how to respond, so he didn't. They finally stopped to camp for the night, and Jam'elo made his standard rounds of the settlers to make sure that everyone was doing fine. For one evening, it seemed, he could rest. He was due to record a log today, and that evening task, as it absorbed him, didn't really remove the sense of unease he had gotten from his conversation with Curtis.

Oregon Trail, July 4, 1859

As Martin rode, he worried about Edwin. He thought back to the moment when they had decided to travel east together. Martin had been sitting at the wooden bar that he knew used to be shiny but had seen better days. The saloon was mostly empty, with just a few madams around, and men like him, with nowhere to go. He nursed his whiskey. It was only 2:00 that afternoon, and he had just lost his job as one of the last guides for the gold mining companies in California. The gold was pretty much all gone, and many companies were folding up, and moving on. There was nothing holding him in California any longer.

His trip to California ten years ago had been a miserable failure. He was ecstatic after his first early find. He thought would save every penny of his finds, and then return to Virginia a rich man, buy a plantation, and build the kind of life that his father lost. But there were no more significant finds. After a few years, he completely ran out of money, and he got hired on as a guide to help companies make their way through the Sierras to places where they might set up a hydraulic mine. And now, that work was beginning to dry up as all of the key spots were claimed.

It was time for him to go home. He missed Virginia terribly, even though he didn't miss his father. He missed the hills and forests near his home and the idyllic plantations. He didn't know if there was a place for him, but Virginia was always home in his heart.

"Martin, I've been looking for you. A bit early to be drinking, isn't it?" Martin had turned to see his tall, lanky friend Edwin. He had met Edwin when he was hired on at the mine run by the Bunker Hill Company.

"Eh, Edwin, why the hell not?"

"That doesn't sound good, Martin."

"They are wrapping up, they don't want me anymore, and neither does anyone else. I miss Virginia. It's time for me to go home."

Edwin nodded. "I can understand. I'm going home to Rhinebeck. My father has wanted me back on the farm for years now."

Martin felt a stab of envy. He wished he had a place to go home to like Edwin did. He pushed the feeling down.

Martin held up his glass of whiskey. "To home."

Edwin held up an imaginary glass and pretended to toast.

"So, Edwin, why were you looking for me?"

"I ran into Julia this morning."

Martin's mood brightened briefly. "Really?"

"She asked me to give you something."

Edwin handed Martin a letter. Martin hesitated, then took it. His mood darkened. He already knew what it said.

"Are you two going to..."

Martin shook his head. "No, it's over."

"What happened?"

"I'd rather not discuss it."

Edwin was quiet. Martin sighed, drained his glass, and got up from the stool.

Martin said, "It's time for me to pack my things, and find my way back to Virginia."

"If you would like a traveling companion, we can travel together to St. Louis."

"I would like that very much, Edwin."

Martin was brought back to the present, and looked over at Edwin, who was slumped in his saddle. Edwin had been sick for days, and he was getting measurably worse each hour.

"Edwin. Edwin!" Edwin jerked up and looked around as if he was lost. He finally looked toward Martin, and when he saw him, it was as if he remembered where and who he was.

"Martin, where are we?"

"We are a few days from Independence Rock. You look bad, Edwin."

"I'll be fine, really, I'll be fine." Martin wasn't convinced.

"Edwin. I'm worried about you. I see a wagon train up ahead—we should camp there for the night, and I'm going to ask them if they have anyone who can help you."

Martin saw Edwin nod slowly, and they picked up their pace.

As they approached the wagon train, which was clearly stopped for the night, Martin could see that it was quite large. He worried a little bit about how they might respond to two single men traveling in the other direction, but he put those worries away, and dismounted to look to find someone who might be able to help.

He saw a young man, who was talking to an older man who looked related to him.

"Hello! Do you happen to have a doctor on hand? We need his help."

The younger man turned and looked at Martin, and Martin could feel his assessment. After what seemed like a long time, he approached Martin.

"Sure, we have a doctor." He looked at Martin's companion.

"He looks pretty sick."

"He is."

"I'll go get the doc."

"Thank you so much!"

The young man ran back toward the wagon train, and Martin got off of his horse, and helped Edwin dismount. He put his and Edwin's blankets on the ground, and had Edwin lie on them, and put his saddlebags behind Edwin's head. He could feel how feverish Edwin was.

The young man returned to where they were, with a strange-looking man in tow, who quickly moved to be beside Edwin. Martin stared at him. He was tall, and dressed normally, but looked kind of like an Indian, but sort of like a mulatto, too. There was something about him that Martin didn't like, and definitely didn't trust. Martin couldn't imagine that he'd have anything useful to offer Edwin.

Oregon Trail, 26 Musb 742/July 4, 1859

Since they had taken a few days off before leaving Independence Rock, the celebration for July 4th was muted. They stopped for camp early, and Jam'elo was making his rounds to check on a few of his patients. Harriet Peterson was very close to giving birth, and Jam'elo was at her side quite often. He walked toward their wagon, and saw Mr. Peterson sitting in front of a fire, stirring a pot sitting on top of it.

"Hello Mr. Peterson. How is your wife today?"

"Ornery as ever. She's really ready to give birth, but the baby seems to have its own schedule."

Jam'elo laughed. "That's the way it goes. The baby always has a mind of its own."

"Anyway, she's over with the other women washing up and changing her clothes. She'll be back in a few minutes. I'm finishing up the rabbit stew if you'd like some."

"That would be wonderful. Thank you. You were one of the last stops on my rounds anyway."

As they ate, they chatted for a while about the day, and the trip so far. Then Mr. Peterson changed the topic.

"Jam'elo, you are not planning to settle in Oregon, are you?"

"I don't know, Mr. Peterson. I'd like to stay for a while, but I also want to see other places."

"You know you aren't allowed into Oregon officially. Someone might arrest you if you decided to stay."

"Mr. Peterson, I am neither a negro, nor a mulatto. I know many think that I am, but I am not. I am a foreigner."

"Well, Jameelo, that may be, but I can't imagine most people believing that."

Jam'elo nodded. Mrs. Peterson came back, and Jam'elo examined her. She was well on her way and doing fine. He took his leave of them and walked further toward the back of the group to another family that he knew he should check up on—the son had a nasty infected toe that he had treated yesterday. He looked up to see Curtis running toward him.

"Jam'elo!"

"Hello Curtis. What's the hurry?"

"There are a couple of men who are traveling in the opposite direction, and one of them is really sick. I told him that we had a doctor with us, and he wondered if they could prevail upon you to help him."

"Of course. Take me to them."

The instant Jam'elo saw the man lying on the ground on some blankets, he could see how sick he was. Jam'elo took out his medical kit, and knelt down next to the patient, to begin his diagnosis.

"Who are you?" Jam'elo turned and looked up to see the sick man's companion looking at him suspiciously.

"I am the doctor. Do you want me to help your friend here?"

Jam'elo could see the man look at Curtis, then look back at his friend.

"What can you do?"

"I can make him better."

Curtis said, "He can, really—he has been treating people on our trip for months. He knows what he is doing."

Jam'elo appreciated Curtis' words, but also resented their necessity. The man still looked hesitant and towered over Jam'elo somewhat threateningly.

"Well, do you want me to help, or don't you?" The man nodded and moved a little bit away.

"My name is Jam'elo."

"I am Martin, my friend's name is Edwin."

Jam'elo turned his attention back to his patient, who at this point was delirious. Jam'elo looked inside his mouth and checked his glands. Yes, agent 24 again. He was getting pretty used to treating it. He took out his antibiotic, and took out his canteen and poured some water in the cap. He put a few drops into the cap, and then put the cap to the Edwin's lips.

"Drink this, please."

Edwin sipped at the cap until it was empty. Jam'elo put the antibiotic and canteen away and stood up.

"He will be better in a few hours and should be ready to travel in the morning. I would like to check up on him before you leave."

Jam'elo could see by the way that Martin continued to look at him that he didn't trust him. It didn't matter. Edwin would be fine by morning. He and Curtis took their leave.

Oregon Trail, 43 Musb 742/July 31, 1859

They had been climbing steadily for many days. Jam'elo had learned from Mr. Thomas that the passage over the mountains this far north was much gentler than the passage further south. They had been climbing over small and larger hills for a long time, and they were headed up into a more mountainous part along a small river. Curtis and Jam'elo were up ahead of the rest of the train, scoping out the trail.

"This river would have a lot more water in the springtime than it does now," Curtis said loudly, as he maneuvered his horse through the rocky trail next to the river.

"How long will we be following this river?" Jam'elo actually already knew this answer, but he was being conversational.

"For a while, I think—past the canyon."

The hills surrounding this river were getting taller and closer in as they kept going uphill, and eventually, they were surrounded by cliffs that were quite high – higher than any Jam'elo had seen so far. Eventually, the canyon opened up, and Jam'elo and Curtis found a very wide spot next to the river that looked like a prime place to spend this night. It was clear that many a train before them had used it.

Jam'elo said, "I'll ride back and let the rest know we found a great spot to camp."

Curtis nodded, and Jam'elo began to turn his horse around, when he felt his horse trip on something. The next thing he knew, he was falling face-first into the ground.

Luckily, he had the presence of mind to move himself away as he was falling, so that his horse didn't fall on top of him. Jam'elo was on the ground, and he could hear his horse screaming. He looked back at his horse, which was on the ground, writhing in pain, and had blood streaming from one of its front legs. Jam'elo could see a piece of bone sticking out of it.

Curtis had dismounted and had taken out his rifle.

"No! Curtis, don't kill my horse!" Jam'elo knew that was the standard treatment; the train had already lost three horses, where people had shot them before Jam'elo could get to them. Jam'elo scrambled upright, and grabbed his medical kit, which had been thrown with his saddle a few feet from the horse. He quickly grabbed the anesthetic and sat down next to the horse's head. He put his arm around his head and put a very large dose of the anesthetic inside of the horse's mouth. After a few minutes, the horse's movements stopped, and he was quietly breathing.

"Jameelo, you can't cure a horse's broken leg."

Jam'elo looked up at Curtis. "Curtis, please go back to the rest of the train, and let them know where we'll be camping. I'll deal with my horse, alright?"

"I know you've done right by people, Jameelo, but a horse with a broken leg?"

"Please, Curtis?"

Curtis nodded and mounted his horse. As Jam'elo could hear Curtis leaving, he got out the things he needed to fix his horse's leg.

First, he used his laser scalpel to open the leg up a little so he could fit as many of the pieces of bone back in place as possible. He took out his solution with nanoparticles that would knit the bone and injected it into various areas of the broken metatarsal bone. He then wrapped the part of the bone that was broken with a dissolving fabric, which would have the effect of keeping the bone pieces in place for the hour or so it would take the nanoparticles to knit the bone completely. He then sutured the skin back together—he thought that if he used the regular method which would leave no scar, it would be too suspicious.

He got up, looking for a stick that was about the right size, and used it and some fabric he had to create a splint. It wasn't strictly necessary:

in about an hour, the horse would be able to walk again, and in a day, he'd be able to support the additional weight of a rider. Jam'elo decided he would keep the splint on the horse for a week or so, and not ride him for perhaps longer, so as to make this a bit less miraculous than it might appear otherwise.

In about an hour, Jam'elo woke the horse up, who then got upright quickly, and began to walk around somewhat tentatively. Jam'elo took the horse to one side of the wide area, and tied him to a small tree, and gave him a little sedative solution that would quiet him down and prevent him from wanting to walk much.

Jam'elo could hear the wagon train approaching well before it arrived. Eventually, they all made their way to the camping spot, and Jam'elo found the Thomas' wagon. Curtis was in the process of helping his mother take out the things they needed for setting camp. Jam'elo wanted to get his larger medical kit so he could replenish his smaller kit from what he used, as well as get some stronger-looking fabric for the splint.

"Hi Curtis, thanks for taking my place in getting the train here."

"Sure thing. Do you think your horse will make it?"

"Yes. I've done a preliminary splint, and I need to grab some things from my trunk so I can make the splint stronger. He'll be able to walk tomorrow, but I won't be able to ride him for a week or so."

"A week? Jameelo, I've never heard of a horse that could be ridden after a break—especially not a break like that."

"Curtis, trust me, I know what I'm doing."

"Jameelo, I know that you know what you are doing —I've seen it enough times. But I don't know that I trust you, honestly."

Jam'elo was surprised, and a bit concerned. "What do you mean?"

"You are so secretive about what you do, and you are better than any doctor I've ever come across—or anyone I've known has ever come across. What's going on?"

Jam'elo sighed. "Curtis, there isn't anything going on, besides that the medical knowledge where I am from is better than here. I'm just using what I know from home."

Curtis nodded but didn't look convinced. Jam'elo would have to be much more careful from now on. He had underestimated how much some people noticed.

"Heave!"

Jam'elo was on one side of the back of a wagon, and Curtis was on the other. The wagon had gotten stuck in a bad rut and broken an axle. They were trying to get it out of the rut so they could get the axle fixed.

"Heave!"

Finally, their combined strength lifted the wagon out of the rut. One of the wheels tilted strongly to one side, and the wagon seemed almost ready to topple.

Curtis shouted, "Get some barrels, or something, to hold up this side!"

Someone managed to get some boxes and barrels in place, and the wagon was no longer in danger of toppling over. Jam'elo stepped away from the wagon and wiped his brow.

Curtis said, "Glad that's over." Jam'elo nodded.

They were in the last month of their journey. They would arrive in Oregon City in about 25 days. They were approaching Mount Hood from the east, along a road Mr. Thomas called the "Barlow Road." It had been built about 15 years before and was well used. Mr. Thomas explained that although there was a toll for the road, it was a far better route than going by river, which was the other alternative.

The road was smoother than in some places they had traveled, but it was rough and rutted in many places. This was but one of several times where wagons needed to be assisted through one portion of the road or another.

Jam'elo looked out at the tall, snow-capped mountain in the distance. It was one of the most spectacular sights he'd seen so far on this journey, although he certainly had seen many sights along the way. He enjoyed seeing mountains and snow—it reminded him of home. He was still enjoying the trip and was unsure what he would find when they arrived in Oregon City. His hope was to find a small community that needed a doctor and start there.

Jam'elo thought this had been a successful expedition so far, and he imagined that he could winter in Oregon, then travel again next summer, perhaps down to California. He had gathered all sorts of interesting information and artifacts along the way and looked forward to seeing what life in Oregon was like.

His relationship with Curtis, however, had changed ever since he had cured his horse's broken leg. In fact, his relationship with everyone in the whole train changed. People still happily asked him for his medical help, but they were much more suspicious of him, and kept their distance. Curtis was polite, but reserved, and they hadn't had much conversation. Jam'elo more often than not rode alone now.

They got back on their horses and rode forward to meet Mr. Thomas at the head of the wagon train.

"Dad, we need to stop for a while. The William's wagon has a broken axle. It will take a while to fix—we're out of the extras."

"OK, son, thanks. Let's camp in that wide field over there for the rest of the day and tonight. Please let everyone know."

Curtis went riding down the line of wagons to share the news, and Jam'elo found a spot that he wanted to set down for the night. Soon, he'd be making his nightly rounds.

Chapter 3

Expedition Log 742.4.21. Student: Jam'elo z Kadarin. Date: 80 Musb, 742

We arrived in Oregon City a few days ago, and the party has broken up. I have been told of a small town south of here, called Canemah, which has had a need of a doctor for a long while. I leave tomorrow to head down there.

Oregon City is a very busy community, with many travelers looking to make land claims of one sort or another, so they can start their homesteads. Some members of our party are settling in and around Oregon City, hoping to be employed by a local mill or other business.

I bid Curtis farewell yesterday. He and his family traveled on southward toward Salem, where Mr. Thomas' brother has a homestead. Curtis suspects that I am different than I claim to be, but he has not pressured me about it, for which I am thankful. But he has kept his distance from me lately, which saddens me. This culture is just in its infancy of understanding concepts relating to space, and I imagine he would think me insane if I told him the truth of my origin.

Attached are climate observations and the final set of activity reports. I have asked my AI to send listening devices to Canemah, and I will be able to do a bit of monitoring of that community in advance of my arrival.

Canemah, Oregon, January 1, 1860/14 Klef 742

Jam'elo finished the stitching of the wound on Gareth's forehead. He laughed internally—he spent more time stitching wounds from bar brawls than dealing with many other kinds of ailments and accidents.

"OK, Gareth. Try not to get in the way of another whiskey bottle anytime too soon."

Gareth grunted, "Thanks, doc." He got up and walked out the door. Jam'elo was left with his thoughts.

It was early in the morning, and while most people in town had been celebrating the New Year, Jam'elo slept. He wasn't much for loud celebrations, even on Casiti, and he didn't quite understand this one. For Casitians, the New Year, which happened only every four Earth years, was a solemn occasion, mostly set aside to honor those that had died the year before, and remember and honor those who died during slavery, hundreds of years earlier. This happy, boisterous celebration seemed strange to him.

So far, his time in Oregon had been uneventful. He had met many people, most of whom treated him well, and all were quite happy to have a doctor on hand. They had given him space over one of the stores, and it included room for him to sleep, as well as practice. He had been reading the local newspaper avidly, as well as getting information from incoming messages at the telegraph office, which was a hub of activity in town.

He was aware of the upcoming election for president, and he was quite curious about the politics of this election. Most people he talked to seemed to think that this election was going to be very important— and everyone had an opinion about what the next president should do about slavery.

He heard a gentle knock at the door.

"Come in, please."

A tall woman, who was neatly and practically dressed, came into the room, carrying a boy child. Jam'elo had seen them before, and he remembered that her name was Mrs. Jameson. She'd come in a few weeks ago asking for help for her son, who had a minor ear infection.

"Hello, Ms. Jameson, how can I help you?"

"You remember my name! The old doctor never could."

"I'm pretty good with names." Jam'elo couldn't help but smile. He liked Mrs. Jameson a lot.

"My son has his ear infection again. The tincture you gave me to put in his ear last month helped so much." She placed his son sitting on the small table next to Jam'elo.

Jam'elo examined Robert Jr. and verified that it was the same infection that he'd had before. Jam'elo thought that perhaps he could strengthen it a little, to make sure the infection didn't come back.

"Just a moment."

Jam'elo had a small walk-in closet that he had re-purposed to hold all of his medical supplies. He had hidden his real supplies within a concealed drawer. The rest of the closet was taken up with bottles of what he thought of as useless medicine of this place, as well as bandages, sutures and surgical instruments that anyone perusing this closet would find familiar.

He prepared a small bottle of the solution that would treat the symptoms of agent 34 and added to it another solution that would eliminate the infection entirely. He always had to be careful—he wanted it to work, but not too well.

Jam'elo took Robert Jr.'s small head in his hands.

"Alright, little one, I'm going to put some drops in your ear. It will be fine." Mrs. Jameson was next to her son, comforting him. Jam'elo finished, and closed up the bottle, and handed it to Mrs. Jameson.

"As before, put two drops in his infected ear every three hours until it runs out." In fact, the dose he had just given would probably take care of it.

Mrs. Jameson smiled as he handed her the bottle.

"Thank you so much, Dr. Jameelo."

Jam'elo nodded and smiled back.

"You are very welcome, Mrs. Jameson. I hope that you have a good day. I'm confident that your son will recover."

"Well, from what I have seen, I'm sure he will. People think the world of you, Dr. Jameelo."

"By the way, Jam'elo is actually my given name. Feel free to call me that—or call me Dr. Kadarin—whichever you prefer."

Jam'elo thought that Mrs. Jameson looked embarrassed.

"Ah, I see. I apologize…"

"No apologies necessary, Mrs. Jameson, I know I have an unusual name."

She nodded her head, slightly inclining it.

"Thank you again. Goodbye, Dr. Kadarin."

She picked up Robert Jr. and turned and walked out of his office. After she left, he replayed in his head a conversation he'd had with Joseph the postmaster. Joseph had taken a liking to Mrs. Jameson after her husband died, but he said that it was clear to him that she wanted no suitors. Jam'elo didn't really know what a "suitor" was, but he figured out that it had something to do with their social process of finding companions, or "spouses" as they called it.

Jam'elo had taken an immediate liking to Mrs. Jameson, but any companionships were out of the question for Jam'elo, until he returned home to Casiti.

Canemah, Oregon, January 1, 1860

Lena shook off the feelings she had as she left the doctor's office. Dr. Jameelo, no Dr. Kadarin, was a sweet, charming man, as well as being beautiful, with eyes that she could get lost in, and a body... She shook off that feeling, too. It would do no good for her to dwell on it. She was insistent that she would stay independent. Besides, she had a different feeling about that Dr. Kadarin. He was hiding something, and she was suspicious of him.

She hadn't talked with him about it, but people said he was from some far away land called "Casiti." Problem is, Lena had never heard of it, and she had studied geography at Mount Holyoke Seminary, where her parents sent her 15 years ago, and she'd heard many a story from her uncle George, who had traveled around the world. She also had lived in France for a few months and traveled around Europe. She had spent countless hours studying the globe, and heard of many faraway places, but Casiti wasn't one of them.

She also thought that what she'd heard about his skills as a doctor seemed a bit... well, a bit too good. That said, she was glad he hadn't been around while her husband was sick. She suspected he would still be alive.

His office was her only stop in town today since everything else was closed. She put Robert Jr. in the back of the wagon with Clara, who had been waiting outside while she was in the doctor's office. She got up onto the seat of her wagon, snapped the reigns, and headed down the road toward home.

Her life had been quiet and mostly full of contentment. She enjoyed the work of the ranch, and loved having enough time to teach the children, and even read and write. Sometimes, she was envious of one of her neighbors, who truly loved her husband – she could tell that they worked well together, and she wished she'd had that sort of relationship with Robert.

They arrived at the ranch, and Lena bustled about doing a few chores, and cooked dinner. After she'd fed the children, and put them to bed, she couldn't help but think again of Dr. Kadarin.

Outside Canemah, Oregon, May 18, 1860/108 Klef 742

Jam'elo felt the feverish forehead of the girl in the bed next to him. She had a very high fever and was a little delirious. He'd already done his diagnostic—she was suffering from agent 24. Agent 24 in children was almost always fatal with the knowledge here.

"How long has she been sick, Mrs. Jameson?"

Mrs. Jameson looked scared.

"About three days. It seemed like she'd been getting better, but suddenly, she took a turn for the worse this morning."

"Good thing you came and got me. I'm going to give her this tincture right now. I'd like to watch her for the next hour or so and see how she responds. If she responds well, I can leave this with you to give her further doses tonight and tomorrow."

Jam'elo tilted up the girl's head and slipped a spoonful of the tincture in her mouth. She swallowed it.

"That's good. It didn't taste too bad, now did it?"

She shook her head, and then after a little bit, closed her eyes. Jam'elo knew his solution was doing its work.

"Dr. Kadarin, since you need to wait for a while, will you have dinner? I have a nice stew and some fresh biscuits."

"That's very nice of you Mrs. Jameson, I'd quite enjoy that."

He stood up and followed Mrs. Jameson into the large front room. It had a fireplace and a large wood cooking stove. In the center was a dining table. Her son, who Jam'elo knew was named after his deceased father, played with some wooden blocks in a corner.

"Please, have a seat. The stew is ready. Robert Jr. and I ate before you came."

She placed a bowl full of a delicious-smelling stew in front of Jam'elo, and a plate with biscuits. She slid a small crock with butter toward him. She sat across from him and was sipping at a cup of tea.

"Dr. Kadarin, I very much appreciate this visit."

Jam'elo was enjoying the stew and had to finish chewing before he spoke.

"You are welcome. It's part of my work here."

"Why did you decide to come to Canemah?"

"I started my travels in Saint Paul, and a friend knew of someone traveling out this way, and I thought it would make a grand adventure. When I arrived in Oregon City, I was told of this town, and its need for a doctor. So I decided to come here."

"This is not the most, well, cosmopolitan place you could choose."

"I wasn't looking for cosmopolitan, Mrs. Jameson. Just a nice quiet place to be a doctor, and, well, observe and learn."

"Where did you say you were from?"

"It's very, very far away. It's called Casiti. I know no one here has heard of it."

"Unlike most people out here, I'm quite learned. I studied geography, and I've been to Europe. But even then, I've not heard of it. That seems a bit strange to me. What is it near? Is it in the Orient?"

Jam'elo felt the stew sit heavily in his stomach. This was the first time that he had met anyone who might be in a position to question what he said about his origins. Unlike the ease with which he and others had seen Earth humans lie, Casitians never learn to lie as children, and his skill with it wasn't very well developed. His best defense was to redirect the conversation.

"Really, it's so far away, and so small, it's not a surprise you haven't heard of it. Where are you from? You have a different accent than many here."

Mrs. Jameson looked at Jam'elo closely. Jam'elo wondered if she were weighing whether or not to challenge Jam'elo about his origins.

"I'm from Richmond, Virginia. My parents have a large tobacco plantation, and I am happy to be gone from there."

"Do you mind if I ask why?"

Again, Mrs. Jameson looked at Jam'elo closely, and Jam'elo got a sudden feeling from her—one of deep curiosity. He was surprised to feel it.

"Dr. Kadarin, what do you think of our country's peculiar institution of slavery?"

"Slavery is always wrong, no matter what the situation. Having one being able to own and control another being is forbidden in our culture."

"Your culture? Is it so different than ours?"

Jam'elo knew he needed to tread carefully, but he couldn't help wanting her to know about him, and who he was.

"It is different, yes. Everyone, including women and men, are treated equally, and there are no slaves. We had an early experience of slavery which taught us quite a lot."

She smiled. "That sounds, well, like a nice place."

"Yes, it is."

"Do you miss it?"

He nodded. "You still haven't told me why you were happy to be gone from Richmond."

"My family owns many slaves. I abhor the practice, but I knew that I could do nothing about it if I stayed, so I did what I could to leave."

"If you don't mind my asking… is that the reason you married?"

She nodded. "It was the only way possible. Women can't travel alone, and I knew that Robert was intent on traveling West."

Jam'elo felt a rush of anger, and then he looked up to see her jump slightly. He didn't think the anger had shown on his face.

She said quietly, "You don't like something about that?"

He took a breath before he answered.

"Mrs. Jameson, I find it horrific that the only way you could change your situation was to get married to someone who you didn't really want to be with otherwise."

She looked at him with a strange look on her face.

"Dr. Kadarin, that is the lot of women in this world. I am surprised that you are… surprised by this."

Another redirection was in order. "Well, now that you are here, Mrs. Jameson, how do you like Oregon?"

She leaned back in her chair. Jam'elo realized he must have insulted her in some way, but he didn't quite know what else he could have done.

"I like it alright. So, if I may ask, why aren't you married? Is there someone waiting for you in 'Casiti'?"

Jam'elo could hear the way she said the word 'Casiti.' It was said as if it was fictional. He thought for a moment. Somehow, he wanted to be honest with her, but he didn't know how to be honest without delving into territory that was quite dangerous.

"No, there is no one waiting for me, really. I am not allowed to have... a companion while I am traveling." He didn't want to use the word 'spouse' since it didn't make sense. The best word he could use was 'companion.'

"Companion? That's an interesting word to use, Dr. Kadarin."

He nodded. "It is the best word for me to use. We don't really... get married in our culture."

She opened her mouth to follow up, but she was interrupted by her daughter in the next room.

"Mother, mother, are you there?"

They both got up from the table, to enter the small bedroom in the back. Clara was sitting up, looking far better than she had just a while ago.

"Mother, I had the strangest dream. But I feel a lot better." She looked at Jam'elo. "Who's that?"

"Honey, that's Dr. Kadarin. He's the one who made you feel better."

"Thank you Dr. Kadarin!" She got up and walked over to him. He bent down, and she gave him a hug.

"Clara let's get you back to bed. I have to examine you."

"I'm fine, Dr. Kadarin, really I am."

Jam'elo realized he'd been far too eager to make her feel better. He'd made the solution too strong.

"You might think so, but you're far from healed. Please lie down."

Jam'elo did a cursory examination and used his diagnostic kit surreptitiously. Yes, agent 24 was virtually eradicated, and all of her vital signs, as well as levels of varied blood cells were back to completely normal. He sighed.

"Something wrong, Doctor?"

He stood up, feeling scared.

"No, no, nothing is wrong at all. Your daughter will recover completely. Please remember to give her this tincture every three hours until it is exhausted. I'd better go and get out of your way. Thank you so much for dinner, and the lovely conversation."

"You are welcome, Dr. Kadarin." She paused. "Actually, may I call you Jameelo?"

"Certainly, you may, Mrs. Jameson." He made his way to the door and could feel her following closely behind him.

As he stepped over the threshold she said, "Thank you again, and please call me Lena."

He turned and looked at her and feeling washed over him. She looked into his eyes, and he found it almost impossible to look away.

"Good night, Lena."

"Good night, Jameelo."

Canemah, Oregon, May 19, 1860/114 Klef 742

Jam'elo was walking down the street when he saw the crowd in front of the telegraph office. He wondered what was going on, and he walked down to stand among the crowd. He saw Gareth and figured that he might know.

"Gareth, what's happening?"

"Abraham Lincoln just won the Republican nomination for president."

"Really? Is that a good thing?" Jam'elo knew that Gareth was a man of strong opinions. It got him into more trouble than Jam'elo thought it was worth.

Gareth shook his head. "He's too popular. He might win the election."

Jam'elo asked, "And why would that be bad?"

"He's a northerner. He hates the South. If he could, he'd grind Dixie to dust."

Jam'elo knew that Gareth was from Mississippi and had traveled to Oregon mostly because he had been too much trouble for his family. He wished that there was someone he could really trust to talk about this—he didn't know what to think.

He didn't really understand what a 'president' did. The best approximation he had been able to come up with was think that it was like the Caraj in one person. But then, there was also two other kinds of councils. One might be like their administrative council, but the other... He had to admit the system was mysterious to him. Perhaps some of his more politically astute colleagues had figured it out.

Canemah, Oregon, June 18, 1860

Lena had put the children to bed, and was sitting up next to the fire, with some tea. She had recently been re-reading a book she had obtained in Paris when she visited last with Robert, just before they left Virginia, before Clara was born. It was a book that always captivated her. It was called 'Psi Cassiopeia' by an obscure French author, about a planet very far away. She had quite a number of books in French that she used to keep her French language skills sharp. But she hadn't read this one in a while.

She read silently, "Au-delà de l'orbite d'Uranus et de Neptune, plus élevé que la région du ciel où brille Sirius..." That translated to "Beyond the orbit of Uranus and Neptune, higher than the region of the sky where Sirius blazes..."

She loved this book. She hadn't read it since before her husband died. They had argued about it. He'd never read it, but when she described the book to him, at first, he simply dismissed it as a fantasy by some "crazy Frenchman." But then he would criticize her for liking it, and even at times called it "from the devil." She was careful never to read it in his presence after that.

During most of her life, she'd look at the stars, and wonder what and who was out there. Most recently, she looked at the stars, and wondered which one Jam'elo was from. That had to be the answer. The more she got to know him, the more she knew he was not from here. She wanted to find out where he was really from.

Baton Rouge, Louisiana, May 1860

Emma had been at her current home for just about a year. She remembered when she'd just arrived. It was evening, and Emma had been sitting outside of the small cabin that she shared with about seven others, all of whom worked inside the house. She had been sitting on a stump, across from Jesse, an old, grizzled man, who was born on this plantation when their master was still a child. He worked in the fields for most of his life, but now that he was blind, he didn't have to work anymore. She had learned a lot from Jesse, and many people said he had the sight—the sight you don't need eyes for.

Jesse said, "Massa don' give no one fourth of July off. He say it's not his holiday. He don' believe in dis country, he say. In fact, he hardly gives us any holidays. We get the day afta Christmas, New Year's Day, and Easter. Dat's all."

Emma had nodded. "I don' care much."

"You don' care much about nothin', do ya? Someone hurt you bad sometime, huh?"

"I lost my daughter."

He nodded. "Yes, you did. She gonna have a hard time, but you gonna be alright."

"What do you mean?"

"Dere ain't nothing you can do about it, girl. You have to start living for yoursef now—dere ain't no one else."

"Why?"

"Why? Don't you want to live?"

"What for?"

"We gonna be free soon—I know it. I know I won't live to see it. And you'll be more than free."

Emma had said, "You crazy. Dey ain't ever gonna free any of us. Dey die first."

Jesse had just nodded his head and spoke. "Yes, they will. But we be free, after."

Today, Emma was busy taking the food from the kitchen into the dining room. Master and Mistress were having a big dinner party, and there was a lot to do. Emma had been moved into kitchen help just a few months ago, and she was good at it.

She hefted the big platter with piles of pork roast, and brought it into the dining room, and placed it on the sideboard. As the guests started to file into the dining room, she filled glasses with water, and started the process of serving the meal.

A tall man with a moustache and beard that she had heard referred to as Captain Bragg started to speak.

"The nomination of Lincoln is the end, gentlemen. If he wins the presidency..."

Emma's Master said, "He won't win—he's not popular enough, Captain."

Another man whose name she did not know spoke up. "I'm sorry gentlemen, Lincoln will win, and when he does, it will be time for us to say goodbye to this country."

Captain Bragg said, "You think the southern states should secede, do you?"

"I've thought that for years, Captain. The North will never let us alone to do as we will with our niggers and create our lives as we wish. And I fear we are going to have to fight to protect that right."

Emma thought that Jesse would appreciate hearing about this conversation. Perhaps he was right. Perhaps war was coming. She didn't know that she could figure out who would win, although Jesse could tell her, she was sure.

A few days later, on one of her very rare afternoons off, since the masters were off being entertained at another plantation, Emma was exploring the land on the western side of the plantation. She liked wandering in the woods and fields alone, and she found herself staring at some multicolored lichen on a tree, wondering about why it was there.

She'd learned, over time, mostly the hard way, to temper the outer expression of her curiosity about the world, but it never altered its inner expression. She hadn't been able to obtain any books, since her current masters didn't read much. She hoped that one day, maybe when she got free, she could find answers to all of her questions.

Canemah, Oregon, June 20, 1860/133 Klef 742

Jam'elo was in his room, arranging and packing the supplies he would need for his trip. Three things had happened to hasten his departure from Canemah. First, a new doctor arrived in town a few weeks ago. He was a relative of one of the townspeople and had claimed to have been trained at one of the elite medical schools on the East Coast. And, he had a light skin tone, or he was "white" as the people here would call it. From what Jam'elo could tell, that meant that Jam'elo was no longer welcome, and the new doctor had said as much.

Just before that new doctor arrived, Jam'elo had a visit by Lena Jameson and her daughter Clara. They had a very involved political conversation, which had led Lena to ask a few too many questions about his origin, questions Jam'elo wanted to answer, but could not risk. He'd tried to answer what he could and deflect what he could not. And it was clear that Lena was developing feelings for him, and he had feelings for her that were not appropriate.

Lastly, he found a small group of men who were traveling to San Francisco, California. Jam'elo had wanted to see that city, so he decided to join their party. They were leaving in two days, and Jam'elo would be ready.

He heard an urgent knock on the door. That was strange. No one had come to see him in days.

"Yes, come in!"

Lena Jameson burst into the room, clearly out of breath.

"Jameelo, I need your help."

"What's going on?"

"Edna's baby…"

Jam'elo went up to Lena and held her shoulders. She was shaking.

"What's wrong?" Jam'elo had been monitoring Edna's pregnancy since the beginning, and everything had been going fine. He hadn't had a chance to check up on her for the last two weeks, since the new doctor was in town.

"He says… he says they'll both die!"

"Who says? Dr. Miller?"

"Yes, he says there is nothing we can do. She's bleeding and in terrible pain."

"Let's go!"

Jam'elo grabbed his medical kit, and they ran downstairs and outside, and Jam'elo got on his horse and followed Lena on her wagon. They quickly traveled the short distance outside of town to the Willard's place. On the porch was Mr. Willard and some of his friends, with Dr. Miller nowhere evident.

Jam'elo asked, "Where is he? Where is Dr. Miller?"

Mr. Willard said, "He left. He said there was nothing he could do."

"He left?" Jam'elo was incredulous. "Take me to her."

Mr. Willard led him inside, and Jam'elo could smell sweat and fear, and the sharp tang of blood. He went to Edna's side. She was feverish, and clearly in terrible pain, and there had been severe bleeding. Jam'elo saw Mr. Willard backing out of the room. It was probably a good idea.

Jam'elo said loudly, "Please, everyone, listen to me. I need a lot of clean linens and some hot water.

Lena nodded, and she and the other women in the room busied themselves. Jam'elo took out his compact medical imager and looked through it into Edna's abdomen. It was a boy, and he was facing feet first, and the umbilical cord was wrapped around his neck, and there was severe hemorrhaging. Jam'elo knew then that the doctor had been right. Under normal circumstances here there was nothing that could have been done. Both mother and son would die.

Jam'elo had avoided doing surgery as much as possible. Jam'elo knew that surgery to remove an infant from the womb was relatively rare in this country, and extremely rare in Oregon, and most doctors did not have the training to do it. However, Jam'elo knew what to do.

He walked up to Lena.

"I need a favor from you."

"Of course."

"Please see everyone else out of this room and stay with me. I'll need you to take care of the baby when he's born."

"When he's...?" She then nodded. Jam'elo felt like she trusted him. She then started to usher the other women from the room.

He went back to Edna.

"Edna, I'm going to give you something to sleep. Don't worry, everything will be fine."

He put two drops of anesthetic on her tongue, and she was quickly unconscious.

"Jameelo..." He looked up to see Lena looking at him.

"The linens are here..." she pointed to the pile next to the bed, "and the water bucket is over there."

"Thank you, Lena."

Jam'elo set to work. He surrounded Edna's abdomen with linens. He doused a small gauze square with his antibiotic cream and rubbed it on her abdomen—that would sterilize it. He took out his laser instruments and tuned his compact imager to the settings he would need to do the surgery. Once her abdomen and uterus were open, he reached in and unwound the cord from the baby's neck, and then lifted the baby from the womb. He cut the cord and handed the baby to Lena on some linens. Lena took the baby, and Jam'elo turned back to Edna. He needed to act quickly because she'd already lost so much blood. He removed the placenta and closed up the incision in the uterus with one of his laser instruments.

As he started on the abdominal wound, he heard the baby cry heartily, and looked over briefly to see Lena cleaning him up. He would be fine. He wished he could close up the wound in the way that he normally could. It wouldn't leave a scar at all. But that wouldn't be appropriate, so he took out some suture, and started to sew the abdominal wound.

He completed his suturing and put away his instruments. He heard Lena behind him.

"She'll be fine, won't she?"

He turned and smiled. "Yes. We should clean her up before I wake her, though—it's a little messy. And I need to examine that one." Jam'elo pointed to the baby in her arms. She handed him over.

"Here you are, sir. I'll get the others in here and we'll clean Edna up." She had a particularly interesting smile on her face, one that Jam'elo decided he rather liked.

He put the baby on the table and did a thorough examination. The baby had a slight case of jaundice, which Jam'elo treated easily, but apart from that, he was a large, strong, healthy boy. Jam'elo then assisted the women in finishing the cleanup of Edna and her bed.

"Well, let's wake Edna up, shall we?" Jam'elo put two drops of the anesthetic antidote on her tongue, and her eyelids began to flutter, and she came awake.

"Edna, you'll be in a little pain in your abdomen for a few days. If you need something for the pain, let me know. You have a strong, healthy son. Here he is."

Jam'elo put her son on her chest, and he could see the tears of relief flowing down her face.

He heard a loud yell behind him and turned to see Dr. Miller and Mr. Willard barging into the room.

Dr. Miller's face was suffused with blood, and he began to shout, "What in God's name is going on here? What do you think you are doing? She's going to die! Get this man out of here!"

Lena stepped in front of Jam'elo.

"Dr. Miller, Edna and her son are fine. Jam'elo was delivering the baby boy you were sure would die. Take a look and see for yourself."

Mr. Willard went to Edna's side, and talked with her briefly, and touched his son. He looked relieved.

Jam'elo said to Lena, "I think it's time for me to go."

Mr. Willard got up, and said, "Thank you Dr. Jameelo, thank you for saving my wife and son."

Jam'elo smiled and nodded. "Of course."

He walked by a stock-still Dr. Miller and went outside to his horse.

"Wait, Jameelo!" He turned to see Lena.

"I need to leave."

"No, please. Don't go. Please don't go. I need to talk to you."

He was worried, but he was also captivated. He wanted to talk with her more than anything.

"OK. Let's talk."

"Follow me to the ranch?"

He nodded.

After the trip to the ranch, they walked into her cabin, and she went to the table and picked up a book.

"Jameelo, have a seat."

He sat down in one of the chairs at the table, and she joined him.

"I want to read you something—well, read you my translation of something."

He nodded, wondering what it was she was going to read. She started haltingly, then began to speak more confidently, pausing on occasion.

"Once extricated from the... vapors of the atmosphere, the abares, which carried... the last of the Nemsedes, and the only... scions of the human race, in their... ascension took on a previously unknown speed."

She kept reading, and Jam'elo then understood what she was trying to tell him.

"What book is that?"

"It's an obscure book written in French. It was published about 8 years ago, I think. I love this book. My husband thought it was devilish."

Jam'elo smiled. "That doesn't surprise me."

"Shall I read more?"

"Sometime, I'd love to hear the whole thing. But not now."

"Jameelo, I saw what you did—I watched you."

"I know. I knew I could trust you, somehow, I knew that you wouldn't panic."

"Even before I saw what you did today, I knew you were different— not from here—I mean, not from this world at all."

He didn't quite know what to say, but he figured he might as well tell her the whole truth. After his story, she looked thoughtful.

"I can see why you didn't want to tell me."

"How could I tell you? Most people would think I was insane."

She smiled. "Yes, they would indeed. But I know better."

"Lena..."

"Don't tell me you are leaving." She got up from her chair and came around to stand next to him. He felt as if he were plunging down a river he could not resist. He stood and she put her hands on his arms. Before he could even think, they were kissing, and he could feel the currents of energy flowing between them. A part of him realized he'd have to explain that, but most of him wasn't paying attention.

Outside Canemah, Oregon, June 21, 1860/133 Klef 742

Jam'elo woke up feeling more peace than he'd felt in a long while. As he opened his eyes, he saw Lena sleeping soundly next to him. He spent a little time watching her, seeing her chest move up and down with her breath, watching her eyelids flutter on occasion. As his eyes wandered away from her, into the surrounding room, the enormity of what he had done hit him, and he sat bolt upright in bed.

He heard her move next to him. He heard her say his name, once, then again. He couldn't move.

"Jameelo! What's wrong? Please speak to me!"

He finally turned toward her and looked into her eyes. She looked worried.

"I've made a terrible mistake. I'm not supposed to..." He felt so distant all of a sudden, and sad at how he was going to hurt her. And how much he was going to hurt.

"Jameelo, I know you can't stay here. And I know I won't want to leave. Do you really think it was a mistake? It doesn't feel like a mistake to me."

Jam'elo sighed. He was deeply conflicted. Every bit of his training suggested to him that he'd made a terrible mistake. But his heart felt otherwise. He looked at Lena and smiled.

"I don't want to hurt you—and I'm afraid I will when it's time for me to leave."

"Jam'elo, I want to enjoy what we have while we have it."

"Well, that is the way of things on Casiti, in any event." He found himself drawn toward her again, and they began to kiss.

"Mother?"

They broke the kiss, and turned toward the doorway where Clara was standing, looking at them. Jam'elo looked at Lena who seemed to be deeply embarrassed, which made him curious. He would have to ask her why later.

"Hi Clara. Your mother and I will be up in a little bit, OK? Are you hungry?"

"Yes, Jameelo."

"I'll make you some eggs."

"Oh, wonderful!" She left the doorway and went into the main section of the cabin.

Lena said, "Eggs?"

"I've been told I make tasty eggs." Jam'elo smiled at Lena. "I guess we should get up?"

She sighed. "Yes. I didn't want Clara to see us."

"Why not?"

Lena had an incredulous look.

"Why not? That seems such a strange question, Jam'elo. Children shouldn't be exposed to that sort of adult... and we're not even married..."

"I can see we have much to talk about. In my culture, it is no taboo for children to know about sex."

They got up, got dressed, and as Lena did varied chores around the house, Jam'elo started a fire in the stove, and made some eggs and bacon, and heated up some leftover biscuits. Jam'elo also roused Robert Jr. and got him to sit at the table. They all finally sat and had breakfast together. Lena was quiet, and Jam'elo was engaging Clara in conversation about the horse she wanted. Robert Jr. finally got up to go and play with his toys. Jam'elo realized it was time to go into town and let his traveling companions know that he wasn't coming with them.

"I'll clean up. I need to go into town in a little bit and tell the travelers I'm not joining them. And then I have to find a new place to stay—Dr. Miller wants my rooms."

"You go, I'll clean up."

Jam'elo shook his head. "No, I'm cleaning up. You have enough to do."

Lena laughed. "Whatever you say. Do all men on Casiti act like you?"

He answered, "Well, pretty much, if I get your meaning. We share all work equally with women."

"Your planet is inexplicably... wonderful sounding. And please... stay here."

"Are you sure? I would like it but..."

"Please, stay here."

He nodded, and got up and collected the dishes, and started some hot water on the stove so he could wash them. He got lost in thought as he finished the job of cleaning up. He didn't quite know how this would all work out, but he was happy.

Outside Canemah, Oregon, September 25, 1860

Lena was finished milking the cow, and she walked slowly from the barn to the cabin. She could see Jam'elo busily splitting wood. She stopped a moment to watch him. Jam'elo was a strong man but wasn't so used to the work of the ranch. Lena chuckled inwardly when she remembered his first try at splitting wood. It was easy to tell that this was not the sort of thing he grew up having to do, but he was getting used to it rapidly. Already, in just a few months, he had become an invaluable help on the ranch, and would make this winter much easier than last winter had been. He had also taught her a lot about better ways to grow vegetables and herbs in her garden.

But of course, his help on the ranch wasn't the most important thing. The most important thing was that being with him gave Lena a kind of joy she had never experienced before. She felt at ease, and truly loved. She could not have imagined that this kind of love existed. It was nothing she'd ever heard of.

Jam'elo stopped splitting and wiped off the sweat of his brow on his sleeve. He looked in her direction and smiled. She kept walking towards him.

"You certainly have gotten better at that, dear heart." The way he smiled always made her heart leap in her chest.

"What is it you say, 'practice makes perfect?' I guess it's true. I want to make sure we have enough wood for the winter. I don't want to be out here doing this in January—I want to be in bed with you."

"That Casitian custom of spending the winter inside mostly in bed sounds like a lot of fun, but not so realistic here. We still have to milk the cows, and take care of the sheep and goats and..."

"I know, I know! No laziness. At least winter is only a few months, not the equivalent of a year."

They laughed together, and she went into the house with the milk. Jam'elo would make butter later. Clara was sitting at the table with one of her primers. She was an early reader and had already gone through a couple of them. Lena hoped that the school that they had been talking about organizing in Canemah would come about, but she wasn't so sure. In the meantime, she would teach Clara herself. Jam'elo had even gotten into the act and was teaching Clara some math and science.

Lena worried a little bit about the influence of Jam'elo on Clara— she particularly worried that Clara might find it hard to adapt to society's standards now that she had been introduced to totally new ways of thinking. But on the other hand, she was happy that Clara got to experience Jam'elo. She hoped that Clara would someday find the kind of love that Lena had with Jam'elo, although realistically, she knew that it wasn't likely.

Sitting on the table was a newspaper from a few days ago— Jam'elo was a bit obsessive about reading all of the paper, and trying to understand what it said, and what it all meant. They had had an interesting discussion last night about the election for the new president. She was trying to explain to him the history of the relationship between the South and the North, and how her parents had been staunchly opposed to the compromises made in 1850. She explained that had caused her brother to become actively involved in Virginia politics. She knew that her brother had been suggesting that the South secede from the Union for years.

Lena was fascinated at how difficult for Jam'elo the whole set of concepts were to understand. He understood slavery—sort of, because of the history of the Casitian people. But he didn't really understand politics, and why people would vie for power and influence. She imagined that he would return to Casiti with a lot of information, but perhaps not a lot more understanding of the system under which they lived.

Chapter 4

Expedition Log 742.6.10. Student: Jam'elo Z Kadarin. Date: 74 Klef 742

It is the Christian holiday of Christmas today. I am learning from Lena Jameson many things about Reit'al traditions. She explained to me that most people in this country celebrate Christmas. I asked her whether indigenous people celebrate, and she said that she thought that many did, that they had been "converted" to Christianity.

She explained conversion to me. It didn't make a whole lot of sense. She grew up with Christianity, but she doesn't feel especially connected to it. Based on what she'd experienced of missionaries and the like she felt like that conversion was often coercive. I had a hard time understanding why it made any sense to try to coerce people to believe something.

As mentioned in log 742.6.1, Lena Jameson has discovered the truth about who I am, I have continued to explain our culture to her. She seems interested and intrigued. Surprisingly, she does not find Casitian culture troubling—on the contrary, she finds it amenable to her points of view.

I have attached my brief essay on what I've learned about Christianity, as well as my most recent recorded interview with Lena Jameson. I am glad that she has been so willing to answer my questions.

Outside Canemah, Oregon, December 25, 1860/74 Klef 742

"Mommy, look at what Jameelo made me!" Clara first held up the miniature wagon, and then she started to play with it. Jam'elo had enjoyed making it. It was intricate, and it had all of the parts of a covered wagon: the wheels and axles, the canopy, the whole deal. He had spent a good part of the last two Earth months making it.

"Yes, Clara, that is quite nice. Jam'elo spent a very long time on it."

"Thank you, Jameelo, I love it!"

Lena said, "Jam'elo, it is beautiful." Jam'elo smiled at Lena. Lena had gotten used to the correct pronunciation of his name. He hadn't had to coach her much; she caught on quickly. He imagined it was because she was fluent in French and Latin—languages were easy for her. His name was pronounced with an almost imperceptible pause between the two parts: Jam – elo, with a long e. Clara, on the other hand, like most people here, couldn't perceive, nor imitate the pause.

He was thinking back on the conversation he and Lena had had about the wagon when Lena first learned she was making it.

"Jam'elo, that is going to be wonderful. Junior is going to love that."

"It's not for Junior, dear heart, it's for Clara. Robert is too young for this kind of toy. He'll break it in less than an hour. I'm making a set of multi-colored block toys for him." Jam'elo had pointed to the pile of wood blocks he had begun to shape.

"For Clara? But... I have been planning to buy her some dolls and a baby carriage."

"Dolls? Those imitation babies and girls? And a baby carriage? Why?"

"Well... that's what little girls get for Christmas gifts."

"Why?"

"Jam'elo, what do you mean why? It's an appropriate gift for a girl. She'll be a mother someday."

"And a toy wagon isn't? Why should Robert be the only one to get a wagon? And he is as likely to be a father someday as Clara is to be a mother. Shouldn't he learn parenting skills? Why doesn't he get some 'dolls'?"

"Well... well... Jam'elo, you have the most infuriating way of destroying the assumptions I've lived with all my life! Now I'll have to think more about this." She wasn't really angry at him, but he could tell that he hit a sensitive spot for her.

Jam'elo and Lena were sitting at the table in the cabin after Clara and Robert Jr. had been put to bed. Jam'elo had finished reading the copy of yesterday's newspaper.

"Lena, the news is disturbing. First, all of these states start leaving the country, and then there is this new conflict in South Carolina..."

"I knew it would come to this. It's much more complicated than the North doesn't like slavery, and the South wants to keep it—but that's not far off."

"Lena, we've talked about slavery—about the Casitian slavery period, and about slavery here. I'm trying to formulate a theory..."

"What kind of theory?"

"Well, one that would explain how humans can take one another as slaves. The Tud'scla were highly protective of other members of their own species. They would never take other Tud'scla as slaves, and they would never attack each other—only alien species. Although I don't think the Tud'scla were at all right, I can understand that kind of culture of species protection. I can't understand how humans can treat each other this way."

"Jam'elo—most people believe that we are the pinnacle of creation—we are all there is. The idea that there are other kinds of intelligent creatures..."

"I understand—you haven't been exposed to that reality."

"And most people... well, white people, think that other races are inferior, not as intelligent or creative or gifted. Some whites, like my parents, even think that we did the Africans a favor by enslaving them."

Lena got up and went to the bookshelf. She took out a volume and handed it to Jam'elo. He looked at the cover. It read *The Inequality of Human Races*. The author was named Arthur de Gobineau. He opened it, and flipped through a few pages, scanning. He then started to read.

"Do people really believe this, that some races are inferior to others, and that the mixing of races is what causes societies to fall?"

"My husband did. It was a hobby of his, this anthropological and philosophical study of the races. It was after he read that book that he decided to move to Oregon, as opposed to the other western territories, because he knew there would be a policy of not allowing negroes into the state."

Jam'elo put the book down. "Honestly, Lena, I have a very hard time understanding this. And, of course, our culture, which is a complete mix of all of the races of humanity and has survived quite well for almost three thousand years, proves this to be false."

"All sorts of things here prove it false, Jam'elo. But that doesn't mean people won't believe it."

Outside Canemah, Oregon, August 10, 1861/5 Hevl 743

Jam'elo had finished the last of the day's wood splitting as the sun went down, and he came into the cabin, smelling a wonderful meal cooking. It turned out that Lena liked to hunt, and she had caught a few rabbits the day before, so Jam'elo assumed rabbit stew was cooking.

Jam'elo had gotten used to eating more meat. It had taken his digestive system some time, early on, to be able to digest meat. He remembered days in the early part of his trek to Oregon when he had to treat himself with an anti-diarrheal. His digestive system had been quite unhappy. In doing a bit of analysis of his own condition, he found that his body didn't have the correct balance of enzymes necessary to digest much meat.

The anti-diarrheal hadn't really lessened his discomfort much, but it did mean he didn't need to stop so often during the trip. Now, his body seemed completely used to meat, and he even enjoyed it. He knew it was a necessary part of the diet here. The agricultural methods that had been developed so far, in growing grains, vegetables and legumes would likely not provide enough calories in this climate, especially given how much manual labor was done.

He assumed that the consumption of fittls, native to Casiti, was what had prevented Casitians from losing the ability to digest meat altogether. They were similar to Earth's fish, and had many of the same amino acids and proteins as Earth meat.

"Smells wonderful," Jam'elo said as he entered into the cabin. Lena smiled.

"Clara and Junior have eaten, and I'm about to put them to bed."

"Jameelo, read me a story!" Clara's plaintive voice was basically impossible for Jam'elo to resist.

"OK, I will. Come, let's read the one about the pony."

"Yay!"

"Me too!" Robert Jr. came running toward Jam'elo.

"I'll read you both a story. You know, Clara, it's time for you to start reading your brother stories—you are getting a little old for this, don't you think?" Clara was almost two Casitian years old, and on Casiti, that was when children began to teach younger children in their family group.

"But I love it when you read to me." Jam'elo could see Clara's pout. He smiled at her.

"I'll still read to you Clara, but you could read to your brother once in a while. It would be good practice."

They walked together to the far end of the cabin, where their room was. Jam'elo helped Robert Jr. change into his pajamas, and he tucked him into his bed. He sat in the chair between their beds and read them the story of the lost pony. It was both of their favorites.

When he finished, he wished them goodnight, doused the lamp, and closed the door. He rejoined Lena in the main room where they sat down to eat, next to each other in one corner of the table.

"It's wonderful getting to watch them grow. I'm glad I get to have this experience."

"Jam'elo, why did you choose not to have children?"

"Mostly, it was because I wanted to go on this expedition. It happens only once every 20 Casitian years. I worked very hard to get the chance to go—few Casitians who want to go get chosen. I guess if I had been rejected by the program, I might have joined a family group."

Lena said, "Honestly, if I really had a choice, I don't know that I would have had children. Robert wanted a son, and he was insistent that I bear children until he had at least one. Luckily, Robert Jr. was my second child. And then, of course, Robert died."

"You've never talk about Robert in a way that suggests that you are sad that he is dead."

Lena gave a short chuckle, then shook her head.

"I am not sad. Life with Robert was rather unpleasant. I know that many women who marry for reasons like mine come to love their husbands eventually. That never happened for me, and I didn't even really like him very much. I'm not sure he thought anything more of me than a brood mare and maid. I have thought that not only do I feel extraordinarily lucky that you came along—I feel very lucky you came along after he died. He would still be alive, now."

Jam'elo nodded. "Yes, he indeed would be. Although it is core to my being to help people who are sick, it would have been sad to me had I known that saving him would have continued your suffering."

"Well, anyway, you are here, now, at the right time." Lena reached over and kissed him lightly on the cheek. Lightly, but with an energy that surprised Jam'elo.

"You've been practicing," Jam'elo said.

"Yes, I have. You can tell?"

"That kiss was evidence. I could feel your desire. You are becoming a very good sender."

Jam'elo had taught Lena all about lyre'es'gkin, the ability for humans to send and receive energy that carried emotion and to some extent thought. Lena had been quite skeptical of it for a while—she thought that Casitians had somehow developed the skill separately from Earth humans, but Jam'elo didn't think so. He thought it was because Earth humans weren't taught certain techniques of mind and heart as children that Casitians learn almost from the minute they are born. Jam'elo had taught some of those skills to Lena, and also to her children.

"I want to ask you something—it's sensitive, though," Lena said.

"Go ahead. I can't imagine what would be so sensitive."

Lena paused, then said, "Well... you mentioned someone named Re'ten, who had been your first companion. I assumed it was a woman, until you talked about a conversation you both had about slavery. I could have sworn you said 'him'."

"What's so sensitive about that? Yes, Re'ten is a man. We were companions in my youth community, I was ... 16 of your years old. He is still a very close friend, and like many people who have been my companions in the past, we still have sex on occasion."

"But…" Lena had a look on her face that was hard to decipher.

"I know that your society thinks that two men, or two women having sex is… what? Wrong? Sinful? What word would you use?"

"Well, many people would use varied words—some think it is a sickness, others think it is a grave sin. It's forbidden in the Bible, and people who practice it are outcasts. Honestly, I've never thought a lot about it, and I never like condemning people for things that I think are their nature, but…"

"Does it bother you that I have had a male companion? Most Casitian men have, at one time or another. I tend to prefer women, but I would never rule out having another male companion."

"No, it doesn't bother me, really."

"What if you fell in love with another woman?"

"That would never happen!" Jam'elo thought that exclamation from Lena had a bit too much fervor.

"Most Casitian women have had a women companion, too."

Lena's brow furrowed. She got up to take their bowls to the sink. "I don't even know what that would be like, or what… But I guess I don't really believe it's evil or sinful. I can't quite imagine living in a society where it is… normal."

"Lena, our society is more different from this one as this one is from any other society on Earth. We had the formational processes of conglomeration of Earth cultures, being enslaved for 2000 Earth years, and then we were exposed to Galactic culture and technology. It is no wonder we are dramatically different. I wish you could visit."

"Me too. But I understand why I can't."

"If they knew what I was doing, frankly, they would whisk me away from here in about five minutes."

"You haven't told them?"

"No. I've withheld from them the fact that we are companions. They seem happy with the information I've been able to share."

"You share information?"

"I send a log entry every six Earth days. If I don't, they will worry about me, and eventually rescue me if they don't hear from me. But there isn't any regular two-way communication, except in cases of emergency."

"Why?"

"Because it is too risky. What would happen if we were sitting here, and all of a sudden you heard this weird sound, and I took out one of my devices that you have seen? Of course, if it wasn't you."

Lena nodded. "Yes, I see what you mean." She smiled. "I think I'm finished talking..." She stood next to him, bent down, and started to nibble on his ear. He stood up and they walked to the bedroom.

Canemah, Oregon, August 15, 1861/16 Hevl 743

Jam'elo walked into the post office, ready to pick up the mail. Lena had ordered some tools, and some toys for Robert Jr. She was also expecting a letter from her mother. As Jam'elo walked in, he saw a number of people he knew. He walked up to the front of the post office.

"Good morning, Joseph. I'm here to pick up Mrs. Jameson's mail. She's expecting a couple of packages as well."

"No packages today, Jameelo, but there is a letter." Joseph went to the back with the mail cubbies, and took out a letter, and handed it to Jam'elo.

"How is Mrs. Jameson these days?"

"She's doing well."

Joseph frowned. "She needs a man to domesticate her. She's been causing trouble." Jam'elo knew a little bit about the political trouble Lena had gotten herself into because of conversations she'd had with various townspeople, some of whom were sympathetic to the Confederacy.

"Joseph, Lena does not need domestication."

Joseph looked taken aback, and said, "How dare you call her by her first name! And how could you possibly know? There are rumors about you two, and you're not helping matters much with your attitude."

Lena and Jam'elo had discussed whether or not they should let it be known that they were involved with each other. Lena had been cautious, and Jam'elo agreed. She didn't care about the propriety of their unmarried relationship, but she did worry that most people thought Jam'elo was a mulatto. Jam'elo couldn't lie about this.

"Joseph, why do the rumors concern you? That is our personal business."

Joseph then stood up, and shouted, "*Your* personal business? I will tell Mrs. Jameson of the evil lies you are spreading about her."

"Joseph, what are you talking about? There are no lies."

Joseph ran out of the post office, leaving customers behind. Jam'elo followed him worriedly.

Lena was inside the general store, and Joseph ran in, shouting.

"Mrs. Jameson, you need to fire that nigger of yours. You need to punish him and send him back to where he belongs."

"Mr. Klyde, what on earth are you talking about?"

"I told him of the rumors spreading about the two of you, and that he needed to put them to rest. He said they weren't lies. He's trying to say that you two..."

"That we what?"

"You are *involved*. I know that is a lie!"

"Mr. Klyde, Jam'elo and I have been in a romantic relationship for over a year now."

Jam'elo looked at Joseph's face, which had become a twisted mask. He glared at both of them, and then turned and stalked out of the store.

On the way home, Lena and Jam'elo talked about what they thought might be the fallout of what had happened.

"Lena, everyone looks at you differently now. I don't understand."

"I don't think you ever will, my love."

Canemah, OR, August 20, 1861/19 Hevl 743

Lena was dressing the rabbits. She'd just gotten back from hunting, and Jam'elo hated dressing the kill. She could understand it— it was something he hadn't grown up with. She hadn't done much of it as a child herself, but she'd seen it plenty of times, and after they had moved from Virginia, it was a task she did herself often. It was easy work for her, and she just set herself to it, and pondered their present predicament.

She had predicted how people in Canemah would react to the knowledge that she and Jam'elo were romantically involved, but she had been surprised at how intense their reaction was. She had been forcefully reminded of that incident when she was a teenager, when she had befriended Jonathon, the son of their cook Katherine. Jonathon had been born on a different plantation and was the son of the plantation owner. When the owner's wife found out about the baby, she forced him to sell them both, and her parents had bought them. She had gotten to know Jonathon over the years and she had even begun to have feelings for him. He was smart, gentle, and always treated her with respect. Not the respect due an owner, but the respect of an equal.

In retrospect, of course, it was all her fault. Once their budding relationship was exposed, Jonathon was given the lash, and then sold. She never saw him again. She hated her parents for what they had done but hated herself more for letting it happen. She'd told Jam'elo of this, and he insisted she was innocent. She didn't believe him. She knew what the consequences would be, but she'd ignored them.

After that, she had always been much more careful around negroes, especially men, fearing for the retribution of other whites because of her, but of course Jam'elo was different. He wasn't negro, or mulatto, but she now knew that no whites understood that at all. Some whites assumed he was free, others assumed he was an escaped slave. No one cared much when he could cure their ills. But once their relationship became known, people were forgetting how helpful he had been, and how many lives he had saved.

She didn't allow him to go into town anymore—she was afraid of what would happen to him. He seemed his same, cheerful, positive self, although she had begun to see that he looked at people differently. And she thought he was less sure about his own physical safety. She was afraid for him, and they had had the closest thing they ever got to an argument. She suggested that he should go home now, because he was in danger. He adamantly refused and was determined to stay by her side until it was his time to leave in about three years.

She was startled out of her thoughts when there was a very loud banging on the front door. She wiped her hands as clean as she could on a towel, and then went to the door to answer it. She opened the door to see two men, one she recognized as the Canemah Sheriff, and one she did not.

"Hello Sheriff Jackson, may I help you?"

"Where is Jameelo Kadarin?"

"Why do you want to know?" Lena knew he was inside, in the greenhouse that he had built, doing some improvements to it. She knew he would be able to hear them. She hoped her tone was such that he knew not to come out.

"He is to be taken back to South Carolina by this man—he says that Jameelo is an escaped nigger."

"Jam'elo has *not* escaped and is *not* from South Carolina. He's not even negro. Where is your proof?"

"I have this note from his owner."

"Let me see it."

The Sheriff interrupted, "I've read it, and I am convinced it is a description of Jameelo."

"I don't care. Show me the note!"

The man she didn't recognize dug into a bag at his side, and gave her a note, from which she opened and read.

"You are clearly mistaken. This note describes a man who is five feet four inches tall and has kinky hair. It describes a large whip scar on his back. The skin tone matches, but nothing else does. Jam'elo has no scars, has curly hair, and is at least six feet tall! Furthermore, this describes a man named Stephen."

"I will be the judge of what matches, and he certainly could have lied about his name."

"If I prove to you that Jam'elo does not match this description, will you go away?"

The sheriff looked hesitant. "I'm sure that it matches Jam'elo, but yes, ma'am, we will go away if it doesn't."

"I will be right back."

She went to the greenhouse and saw Jam'elo standing still. He'd been listening.

"What do you think?"

"I think I should go out there and show them."

"I agree. After this, you are leaving."

Jam'elo shook his head, and Lena could tell he was going to be stubborn. He left the greenhouse, and she followed closely behind, but then grabbed him.

"Let me be between you and them." He relented.

"Here he is. Does he look five foot four to you?"

"No ma'am."

"Does he have kinky hair?"

"No ma'am, I admit he does not, but that is not enough."

"Do I need to show you his back?"

"Yes, ma'am, you do."

Jam'elo slowly took off his shirt and turned so that his back faced the sheriff and the bounty hunter.

"Sorry Jacob, I guess this isn't your man."

The two of them walked out the door, and Lena slammed it in anger.

"Jam'elo, you are in danger, and I will not let myself be responsible for hurting another man."

Jam'elo held Lena's hands. "Lena, you are not responsible. You weren't responsible for Jonathon, and you won't be responsible if I get hurt. Other people are responsible. You are only showing love."

"But Jam'elo, I know what this world is like, and you don't, not really. I know what people do. It is negligence if I let you stay with me."

Lena could see the tears forming in his eyes. She'd seen him cry a number of times—far more than any man she'd ever known.

"Lena, I don't... I don't want to leave you. I don't want to leave you, Clara, or Robert before my time is up."

Lena knew that in the end, she could refuse him nothing. She hoped that didn't lead to anything horrible happening to him.

"There is only one answer, then."

"And that is?"

"We're leaving. I'm going to sell this ranch, and we're going to San Francisco. It's big enough, and has enough people, that no one will notice us. You'll be as safe there as you will be anywhere."

Chapter 5

Lena Jameson has decided to move to San Francisco, California. Since I had originally wanted to travel there, I have agreed to go along with her and her family and assist them during the trip, and likely stay with them. We will travel by stagecoach for the trip, first to Sacramento, then on to San Francisco. I am excited to see more of the western part of this continent and meet new people. Perhaps I will even be able to be of service again as a healer.

Lena Jameson sold her ranch to a young couple that had moved from Ohio. My understanding is that she received a substantial amount more for the ranch than her husband had paid for it seven years ago. I don't really understand why—it has something to do with demand for land here in Oregon—people will pay more over time for the same amount of land.

I'm working on an essay about land ownership. I remember a conversation I had with Elsu, an indigenous man, about land. Apparently, they don't really understand land ownership, either. I hope to continue to talk with indigenous people as we travel and when we arrive in San Francisco. Until the settlers came, they lived much like they lived when the Tud'scla took people from this continent.

I have attached an essay which explores a new model I have of the racial dynamics present in this country at the current time. I describe an uneven relationship between those with light skin, who are in power, and others. I hope it will be an interesting addition to the dialogue around the current situation here. I have also attached the standard climate data.

"Clara, please put everything of yours in this chest." Jam'elo carried the chest for Clara's things. "Everything should fit in here."

Clara was pouting. "I don't want to pack."

"Clara, you don't want me to pack for you, do you? I'll misplace everything, and you'll never find it all later."

"I don't want to leave."

Jam'elo sat down on the floor next to Clara and took her hands into his.

"I know it's hard, little one. But we will be with you, and Junior, too. It will even be fun!"

"Fun?"

"Yes, you'll get to see the ocean!"

"The ocean?"

"Yes. Where we are moving is near the ocean."

"I've always wanted to see the ocean."

"Well, then, little one, better pack." Jam'elo gave Clara his best smile, and then started to pack Robert Jr.'s things in a different chest. He was out in the main room playing while his mother packed.

He finished the packing, and looked at Clara, who was busily putting her things rather haphazardly in the chest. He went out to the main room.

"I got Clara to pack, although I'm far from convinced she'll be able to find anything when we arrive."

Lena chuckled. "I'm far from convinced *I'll* find anything when we arrive." She paused and took a breath. "I'm glad we're doing this, Jam'elo. I've always wanted to see California anyway, and I was getting tired of this small town. And we'll be able to get a nice house; I was gratified by the offer I got on this ranch. I guess there was more demand than I realized."

They worked together in companionable silence. They were leaving in two days and had to have everything packed. Jam'elo noticed that she had set aside *Psi Cassiopeia* to put in their personal luggage. A while ago, she had finally read the whole of the book in translation to Jam'elo. He then told her she should publish an English translation. She laughed and said, "Who would publish an English translation of an extremely obscure French book that most people think is crazy? And who would publish said translation *by a woman*? I would have more luck becoming president."

Northern California, September 15, 1861

Lena looked at Jam'elo, who was sitting across from her in the stagecoach, nodding off into sleep. She was surprised he could sleep—the coach was cramped, and the ride bumpy. They had picked up some new passengers in Red Bluff and would be in Chico by tonight. It had been a tiring trip, but both Clara and Robert Jr., who sat on her lap for the entire trip, thought of it as a grand adventure, encouraged by Jam'elo.

They had decided to pretend that Jam'elo was Lena's employee—it seemed the most prudent course for them. But when they could stop for the night, they shared a bed, which was a comfort to Lena. Other passengers had been largely suspicious of Jam'elo, although he had already been an invaluable help during the trip.

She was looking forward to San Francisco—she could imagine their life among people who wouldn't care much about who they were. She imagined Jam'elo might even be able to find work in a hospital— something he had been so far unable to do.

Lena looked at Jam'elo's face again and felt the warmth of her love for him. She still sometimes was surprised by his love, and his presence in her life. She didn't know what it was she had done to deserve it. She chuckled internally. It certainly had already caused her some trouble, and it would cause her great pain in the end, when he had to leave. But she knew it was all worth it.

She worried a little about her daughter. Clara was growing into a firebrand, and she imagined that life in California would be good for her. Lena wanted her to have opportunities that she'd never had. She even hoped she would be able to vote someday. Robert, at five, was showing a capacity for mature emotional expression that Lena sometimes found disturbing, but mostly made her happy.

Jam'elo seemed to be enjoying teaching both of her children the Casitian mental and spiritual techniques. He is teaching Clara math and science, and Jam'elo is being a trooper, and learning to write English along with Robert. Lena laughed when he told her that he'd never learned to hand write any language, even Casitian. She could hardly imagine such a world.

San Francisco, California, September 25, 1861/56 Hevl 743

It was late evening, and Jam'elo and the carriage driver had finally hauled the last of their bags and chests into their new dwelling in San Francisco, and Lena was busy unpacking. He thought he should keep the children busy while she worked.

They had decided to rent a house first, and this house seemed serviceable. It was located on Kearny Street, in a fairly busy part of the city. Lena was right, no one paid much attention to them, and no one seemed to care who they were. There were people of many different origins here. They had already seen a number of Mexicans and Chinese, as well as free Negroes. Jam'elo would not stand out here.

Jam'elo wanted to find a place where he could practice healing. Even though he knew that San Francisco had a broader range of people than anywhere he had been before, he was not under the illusion that a hospital that treated whites would hire him. He was going to ask around for the places that treated others. He imagined his skills would be appreciated somewhere.

"Jameelo, where is my chest? I want to play with my wagon," Clara's plaintive voice let Jam'elo know that what she really needed was to get some sleep.

"Clara, it's your bedtime, sweeting. Let's find Robert Jr., and I'll read you both the story of the lost pony."

"I don't want to go to bed!" Jam'elo thought that Clara had inherited a good dose of Lena's strong-willed nature.

"Do I have to pick you up and carry you there, then tie you down?" He was smiling. She knew he would do nothing of the sort.

She pouted but walked back toward their bedroom. Jam'elo grabbed Robert Jr. from the floor near where Lena was unpacking, gave her a quick kiss, and then realized belatedly he had no idea where the lost pony book was. Maybe he could get them to sleep by telling them a story, instead.

When they both were in bed, he started his story.

"Once upon a time, there was a very brave girl. She had been born into a family who were serving the Tud'scla. Remember them?"

Clara nodded. Robert Jr. was already asleep.

"This girl had overheard a revolt and escape plan while she was working in the fields. She went home, and told her parents, but they wouldn't listen to her. They were scared and didn't want to make their masters upset.

"But the girl was determined to get her family free. The next day, she approached someone who she'd overheard, and asked to join them. They were skeptical, but she was very convincing."

"Jameelo?"

"Yes, little one?"

"How old was she?"

"Just a little older than you. She was... 13."

"Keep going."

"So late one night, she snuck out of her parent's house, and left them a note about where she was going, and she promised she would come back for them when she could.

"The revolt was only a partial success. She escaped, but she wasn't able to come back to get her family. It made her very sad. But she was strong, and determined, and she tried and tried many times. Finally, about 10 years later, she led the revolt that freed all of the people in her community, including her parents. They all lived happily ever after on my planet."

"Jameelo, when was that?"

"Many, many years ago, little one. Way before I was born. But you can grow up to be a strong girl like that."

He smiled, tucked her in, and doused the lamp.

"Goodnight little one."

"Goodnight Jameelo"

San Francisco, California, October 15, 1861/72 Hevl 743

Jam'elo shook the man's hand. "Thank you, sir. You won't be disappointed in my work here."

The tall and somewhat pudgy man with a greying bush of a beard said, "We need all the help we can get. We lost 3 doctors to that new German hospital on Brannan. The city has a shortage, and, of course, it is these people who suffer."

Jam'elo liked this man, now his boss. His name was Benjamin Morris, and he had started a small hospital near the wharves, where a lot of workmen and immigrants were being treated. He seemed to have a genuine desire to help people who could least help themselves, even at his own expense. The hospital was far from profitable, and he had told Jam'elo that much of the funding came from his own family holdings.

They left his office, and Benjamin showed Jam'elo where he would be practicing. He got to work organizing the space and gathering the supplies he would need. He would mostly be using local medical techniques and medicines, although he knew in some cases, he would be unable to resist using Casitian technology. He would have to be very careful.

After a busy first day, he walked outside to where his horse had been tied up. He decided he wanted to walk for while on his way home. He untied his mare and started to walk down one of the streets toward home. The sun was setting, and a chill was in the air. Jam'elo liked the chilly air in San Francisco during the summer. Everyone complained, but it reminded him of early summers at home, before the weather got truly warm, during the brief days at the height of summer.

As he was walking, he was lost in thoughts of home, and he almost stepped in a large pile of horse manure on the side of the road. He began to walk around it and looked up to see four young men with light skin color standing in his way, staring at him.

One of them spat, and another one said, "What are you doing in this neighborhood, nigger?"

Jam'elo sighed inwardly. He didn't know the city and had simply taken the most direct route home.

"I am on my way home. I live up on Kearny Street."

"Kearny, eh?"

Jam'elo decided that the best strategy was going to be to get on his horse. He backed up a few paces and mounted.

"If you'll excuse me, I need to get going."

As he rode past them, he heard the epithets, and filed them away. He had to admit that he would certainly miss Lena greatly when he finally left to go home, but he would be happy to never have to experience this sort of thing again.

Yorktown, Virginia, April 5, 1862

Martin's first battle, the battle of Manassas, had been a scary one. They had started in Richmond, Martin's old home, and were marching north, because they had heard that the Union Army was trying to strike an early win and take over Richmond. Martin had never been in such a chaotic situation, but he had managed to survive, at least.

Tomorrow was going to be yet another battle. He was getting a bit more used to them, but they still scared him. Martin sat down heavily on a stump, holding in his hand a battered metal bowl, full of some stew made of unrecognizable elements. He thought to himself, "no wonder they call it mess." There was a fair bit of chaos around him. Men were moving things around and shouting to one another. They would be moving out at first light tomorrow. Martin had already packed everything he needed.

A young man named Jason came to sit by him. Martin could swear that Jason was too young to fight.

"Well, Martin, ready for the march tomorrow?"

"I guess as ready as I'll ever be. You?"

"I'd be lying if I said I wasn't scared. But I know how to shoot my rifle, and stab the enemy, so I guess I'm ready."

"You from Richmond, too?"

"Yeah. My dad is a blacksmith in town. I'm going to miss being there."

Martin didn't really have much of a home in Richmond, and his father certainly hadn't wanted to see him at all. He'd come back from his time out West, and had done some odd jobs around town, and rented a small room in a rooming house, but still hadn't hit his stride. The ideas he had of making himself rich somehow had not materialized.

The minute Virginia had seceded from the Union, Martin signed up for the Confederate Army of the Potomac. It seemed the right thing to do. He couldn't quite have imagined doing anything else. Dealing with the occasional Indian or rogue mountain man in his travels in the West was not preparation for what he was experiencing during this war.

He finished up his dinner, and finally lay down, but spent a sleepless night. The next morning, he lined up with the rest of his regiment, and they marched out, and then split up with the orders of the officers.

He was part of a small group that had been ordered by General Magruder to move around from place to place, so that the Union army would think that Magruder's force was much larger than it was. He spent the afternoon with a small group of soldiers, running around, shooting, then quickly leaving. At one point, he could see that a unit of the Union army had pushed forward and were attacking. Martin could hear shouts from the officers, and their plans were in complete disarray.

The noise of the guns around him felt deafening, and the smoke was making him choke. He could see the group ahead of him, and his lieutenant was shouting something, but he couldn't hear it. As he was loading his rifle, he felt this searing pain in his head, stomach and his arm, and then blackness overtook him.

Williamsburg, Virginia, May 6, 1862

Martin was in a line of men waiting to get a medal pinned on his chest: a medal he was sure he did not deserve. Yes, he was part of that early force that had helped convince the Union army that they were a big force and helped win the battle. But he had been badly injured in the first exchange of artillery between the two armies and had missed most of the siege. He had lost his right arm up to the elbow. He would never fight again.

As he stood, hearing the voice of Major General Magruder in the background, he fought the tears of frustration and anger at his circumstances. Every time he tried to do something significant, he ended up losing somehow: losing money searching for gold, losing the love of his life, losing his arm fighting for his home. The pride that he might have felt wasn't there. In its place was the dust of disappointment.

San Francisco, California, May 2, 1862

Lena hadn't written much to her mother since they had arrived in San Francisco. The first letter she sent to her mother had resulted in a response filled with invective. Her mother could not understand why she had moved her family to San Francisco after having been on the ranch in Oregon. Of course, she could not explain the real reason they had left Oregon, but it didn't matter—she knew her mother wouldn't understand that, either.

Her mother had waxed on about how proud she was of her son, Lena's brother, who had joined the Army of Northern Virginia, to defend the South against the "war of northern aggression." Lena saw it as an unfortunate, but necessary conflict to finally end slavery, and she hated the fact that her brother had joined the Confederate army.

Lena sat at her desk, the paper still blank, the pen laying there, with the ink getting dry. She hadn't known what to say to her mother, and how. She gave up. She closed the ink well and stood up. She remembered Jam'elo was cooking dinner tonight—she would go to the market and get some meat and vegetables.

San Francisco, California, August 1, 1862

Jam'elo stopped his horse at their house, got off, and took the horse around the back to the stable they shared with a number of other houses on the block. He put his horse in her stall, and gave her some oats, and brushed her down.

It had been a long day. There had been some sort of disturbance, and five people with stab wounds of varied seriousness had been rushed in. Luckily, they had been able to save all but one. The one who died hadn't made it to the hospital in time. Jam'elo doubted that he would have been able to save him unless he had been on a Casitian ship, where he could have been put in stasis while being treated.

He loved his work and had been learning an incredible amount about this culture, but he missed Lena. He didn't get to spend anywhere near as much time with her as he would like. He missed those days on the ranch when they could spend most of their time together. But this was the best thing for him to be doing: to learn as much as possible.

He walked up the back stairs to their house and saw Lena in the window of their kitchen. He stopped a minute to watch her. He sometimes found it hard to believe the situation he was in—living fully within this society, deeply in love with a woman, helping to raise her children... although he knew that it was against the rules, there was a way it felt somewhat fated to him.

He shook off the feeling and walked in the door.

"Jam'elo, my love. You are home."

"Jameelo! Come see what I did!" Clara's voice rang out from the living room.

"Just a moment little one," Jam'elo called out to Clara. He kissed Lena.

"Yes, I'm home. Happy to be home, my dearest. What's for dinner?"

"I picked up some fish, and I figured I'd try making fish and chips—I loved that when I was in London. I think I might be up to it."

"I'll trust you." Jam'elo smiled.

"Jameelo!"

Lena said, "Her highness is impatient."

Jam'elo chuckled. The first time she'd used that reference he had to ask her what she meant. Now he understood, and he thought it fit. Clara was growing up to be headstrong and demanding. He did hope that she would be able to temper that at some point. He knew that in this society, a headstrong, demanding woman would have a difficult time.

"Coming!" He walked into the living room, to see Clara with papers spread out around her. "What are you up to, little one?"

"I'm working on that puzzle you gave me."

Jam'elo looked at the papers and saw that she had come up with some very novel ways to solve the puzzle. She'd in fact solved it three different ways. Jam'elo smiled.

"That's very good, Clara. You solved that puzzle three different ways!"

She looked up at him and smiled. "Teach me another one like this?"

He sat down cross-legged next to her, and took a blank paper and pencil, and started to draw.

Dallas, Texas, November 1862

Martin always felt that he had been cursed in life. Martin's father had been quite wealthy—an owner of a large plantation in Virginia. His father's young life was full of promise. He had married a prominent politician's daughter and was on his way to greatness. But the depression of 1807 had completely wiped out his father's wealth, due to some ill-advised investments, and he never was able to recover. Martin was the youngest son and was born to a pauper with nothing. Martin's mother had died soon after Martin was born, and his father didn't really know how to raise children. Martin was raised mostly by his elder sister. He left home as soon as he could, to start his own life, and moved West as people moved West. He was a superb hunter and tracker and would guide travelers and settlers on the frontier. He went to California for the gold, found little, and while there he had courted, and lost the love of his life. He returned home empty handed, to do menial labor in Richmond until the war started.

He joined the Army of the Potomac in 1861, and lost his arm in the battle at Yorktown, and could no longer fight. Major General Magruder seemed to like him and had hired him for varied guiding and courier jobs. When Magruder did so badly at Malvern Hill, General Lee moved him to Texas, and Martin followed.

Later, Magruder got too busy for him, and Martin needed to find another way to make a living. Somehow, going home again empty handed didn't feel like an option. He'd finally found a niche: helping people travel through the South, navigating around the conflicts. He was on his way to see a possible new client.

Martin walked into the bar below the hotel, and the stale beer and smoke assailed his nostrils. He hoped he wouldn't have to be here too long. He searched the faces for his friend, Benjamin, who had the client that Martin hoped to guide to Mississippi. He finally saw Benjamin sitting at a table in the back with a slight, clean-shaven man who looked to be in his thirties. He walked toward them and took a seat at their table.

"Martin! It is a pleasure to finally see you after all of this time. I need to thank you for that favor you did last month for my father – finding and bringing his nigger back."

"Ben, it is good to see you as well, and that wasn't so hard. She was easy to find. You look like you are keeping yourself healthy." Martin patted his belly with his one hand. Benjamin had definitely filled out some since they'd last seen each other.

Benjamin laughed and nodded. "Martin, I would like you to meet Edward Hiller. He and his family need to return to their home in Biloxi. Edward, I would like you to meet Martin. War hero, friend of generals, and the best guide I know."

Martin inclined his head. "Nice to meet you Mr. Hiller."

"Nice to meet you Martin. Benjamin here tells me that you are able to get people into and through Union-held territory. You know, they have been holding Biloxi for some time now. How is that possible since you are a Confederate hero?"

Martin smiled. "I'm not really a hero—Union people don't know me, and I have friends everywhere. Mostly, though, you just need to know the right things to say, and the right people to bribe. My fee will be five hundred. How are you traveling? You have a wagon? Horses?"

"We have a wagon drawn by two draft horses, as well as three mares, a stallion and a gelding. We have five negroes."

"That's quite the entourage, but it's not a problem. When would you like to leave?"

"My wife is doing some last-minute shopping. We should be able to leave on Friday. Does that work?"

That gave Martin some time to do a few of his own errands.

"That's fine. Where are you staying?"

"We're staying here."

"I'll meet you here first thing in the morning on Friday."

They shook hands. Martin made as if to move on, but his friend Benjamin put his hand on Martin's shoulder.

"Stay a bit, Martin. I wanted to ask you about what you think about how your Major General Magruder is doing here in Texas."

"It seems that he is comporting himself well. I'm sure he will do fine here."

"Well, after that disaster of Malvern Hill..."

The smells and noise were beginning to oppress Martin. "I'm sorry, Benjamin, I must go. It is good to see you. I'll see you Friday, Mr. Hiller." He got up quickly and moved as fast as he could out of the room, into the fresh air.

San Francisco, California, December 15, 1862

It was late afternoon, and as she looked out of the window that was in front of her small writing desk, she could see the sun in the middle of its early winter's journey to the horizon. The sky had already taken on that tinge of dark blue, and the sun lessened in brightness as she saw it just above the rooftops of the houses across the alley from her.

She looked at the handwriting on the envelope: her mother's careful script. She wondered what her mother would have to say to her this time. The last time, it was to continue to harangue Lena about the impropriety of her decisions. Lena was enjoying her time in San Francisco, and her mother insisted that her place was back in Virginia, on the plantation, especially now that Lena was a widow.

Lena steeled herself, and carefully turned the letter over, and used her slim opener to unhook the sides of the envelope from each other. She pulled out the single sheet of parchment and could smell the slight scent from her mother's favorite perfume, imported at extreme expense from Paris. Lena noticed at once that the letter was very short. Short letters from her mother were quite unusual, and always suggested that something dire had happened. The date on the letter suggested that it had taken it's time to reach her. She read the letter slowly, with trepidation.

Her brother had died in the Battle of Antietam, in September, after joining the Army of Northern Virginia. This letter told her that her father had recently died of a disease she was sure Jam'elo could have cured. Her mother's simple request: "Come home and take care of me."

Lena stood up and paced the living room. She'd moved out West to avoid the plantation—avoid dealing with the realities of her family's life. She'd done her best to avoid it—marrying someone she didn't even like just because she knew his dreams were Westward, not Southern. Moving back to Virginia to take care of her mother, and by extension, the plantation her mother now owned, seemed impossible to Lena. She couldn't even imagine it—but she knew she had no choice in the matter. It was inescapable. She'd have to face the life she'd worked so hard to avoid.

She read the letter again and again, still not really believing it, and still knowing its truth. She was a little surprised at her lack of mourning for her father. She'd never been close to either her brother or father, mostly because they had relished a kind of life that she despised.

And leaving to go back to Virginia meant an end to her time with Jam'elo. He couldn't travel there with her, and he couldn't be with her in Virginia—there just wasn't a way from here to there. She knew he would understand—he could spend time traveling a little bit before it was time for him to go back to where it was he had come from. But the sadness of their imminent parting started to form a knot in her chest. How could she leave him—a man she had come to so deeply love?

Jam'elo was at the hospital. He had been hired by a small hospital that treated indigents, Negroes, Mexicans, and Indians. He had been a godsend to them and he worked very long hours. She was glad that he had found a place, even though she didn't see him as much as she would like to; she knew he was learning a lot by doing that work. She was happy for the time being in San Francisco, but she was sure she would start a new ranch up north after he left. She wanted to raise her children in the country, not in the city.

She didn't know what to do. Jam'elo could not return with her to Virginia. She could say no. She could refuse to return, but that didn't feel right to her. Her mother needed her, and she would comply. And it would mean she would have to say goodbye to Jam'elo.

She got out pen, paper and ink, and started to write the response to her mother.

Dearest Mother,

It is with the deepest sadness that I write you, hearing of the death of my dearest father. I know that both these deaths have come at the most inopportune time.

I have been quite busy establishing myself in San Francisco and was preparing to find a place up north in Sonoma County to start a new ranch. I will postpone that for you and travel east to Virginia.

I don't know yet when I can leave, and I must carefully plan my travel, given the current conflict. I will write you again when I know more specifically when I will be leaving, and by what route I will be traveling.

I hope that in the meantime, you find support where you can, Dear Mother. Know that my prayers are with you.

Your loving daughter,

Lena

San Francisco, CA, December 16, 1862/81 Paqn 743

Jam'elo had never seen Lena so angry.

"You are *not* traveling with me to Virginia! I will not have it!"

"Lena, you are not being reasonable."

"What do you mean, *I* am not being reasonable?"

"You cannot travel alone with your children to Virginia. It's dangerous."

"And you cannot travel to Virginia at all!"

"That's not true. I can travel with you."

"And how is it that we can avoid the inevitable questions, and bounty hunters trying to grab you and sell you?"

"We pretend you own me."

"What? I hate that idea—I hate the idea of you being a slave. It was bad enough pretending you were my employee during our travel here. And do you really think we can pull that off? What about Clara and Robert Jr.?"

"We can explain it to them carefully, and make sure they talk to as few strangers as possible."

"Jam'elo, I love you, and I don't want to say goodbye to you one second earlier than I have to. But I would never, ever forgive myself if something happened to you."

"Lena, I have resources. I have people who are aware of what's happening, and I have ways to contact them in an emergency. I will make sure that they understand the possible dangers of this trip. They will be ready.

She sat down in her favorite chair and looked at him.

"Jam'elo, I seem to be unable to refuse you. On one hand I wish I could call your people myself and tell them to come get you. On the other hand, I am happy you want to travel with me—I can't stand the idea of you leaving too soon. I don't know what I am going to do with you!"

He knelt in front of her chair and put his head in her lap. "I know you fear for my safety, but I will be fine. And I will not leave you to travel into the South without help."

He looked up at her and could see that her features had softened. She tilted her head slightly and put her hand under his chin.

"Ah, Jam'elo. You are the love of my life. I shall never meet your like again. Come to my bed. If we are traveling as you suggest, we have few nights left where we can be together without care."

Baton Rouge, Louisiana, August 1862

Emma was lying in the middle of the meadow, as she often did at night, looking at the stars. It was her comfort, her love. She had learned many of the constellations over her life, and she knew which ones were winter constellations, and which came up in summer. Her favorite had always been Orion, but that wasn't up now. There was something about that constellation—some kind of strength that she got in looking at it. Tonight, there were a lot of shooting stars—she loved to be outside for them. She was glad it was a clear night. As she watched the stars, she wondered what it was like up there—what it might be like if she could actually be up there. She wished she had her astronomy book. It was taken from her when she was auctioned off.

Her life had settled down. Her new master wasn't so bad, and the life was pretty easy. She missed her daughter, and often wondered how she was, but she had resigned herself to the fact that she would never see her daughter again. It wasn't unusual—she'd known many women who had lost their children, or husbands. As Jesse said, it was time to live for herself.

She had spent some time determining how easy escape would be, but Jesse had been telling her for months to bide her time—there would be the right moment, he said. She was willing to listen to Jesse—for a while at least. But now that she didn't have anyone to take care of anymore—she wanted to find her freedom. She knew that she would, somehow. Jesse had told her a month or so ago to get ready, and she had made many preparations.

A few nights later, Emma was awoken by sounds of gunfire. She'd been prepared: Jesse had told her that he had heard that the Union army was coming this way a few days ago. She was always surprised by what Jesse knew—given that he was blind and never traveled far from the cabin. A few days ago, Jesse had told Emma that she needed to take this opportunity to find her way to freedom. And she knew Jesse was right—this was the best opportunity. There would be chaos, and she expected that her master would be busy with other things. She had prepared a small bag, and a bedroll. She'd squirrelled away beef jerky, cheese and biscuits. She was just waiting for the right moment.

She heard shouts, and she came fully awake. She put on a shawl and walked outside of the cabin. She could see in the distance the main house, and a column of soldiers coming down the driveway. Jesse had said that the Union soldiers often took over plantations to use them as staging grounds, and to get food and other resources. She realized that this was the moment she was waiting for.

She went back into the cabin. None of the other slaves wanted to leave with her. They were scared that they might be caught or killed by Confederates. Emma was determined to get out of there and get as far away toward the west as she could.

She got dressed in the tight undershirt, shirt, jacket and pants that she had managed to obtain a few weeks ago and took the bag she'd prepared and the bedroll. She had decided, without Jesse's help, that the best way for her to travel was to pretend she was a man. Her breasts were small, and she had a slim frame, so she knew she could get away with it. She would tell people her name was Edward, and she had left a plantation that had been razed by the Union Army.

She went to Jesse, who was sitting in the corner of the cabin.

"I'm leaving now, Jesse."

"Good, good. I'm glad you gonna get out of here girl. Go, don' spend no more time wit me—get yoursef out of here."

"Bye Jesse, thank you for all you have done for me."

He looked at her with his unseeing eyes and smiled. "You'll do fine. And you'll meet a man who can help you. I promise."

"A man?"

"He a strange man, a man from the sky. You'll first see him as a slave—but he ain't no slave. He from the sky. He help you, I promise."

She walked out of the cabin into the night with those words ringing in her ear. A strange man? She'd see him first as a slave, but he's not a slave? She didn't understand what all of that meant, but she was happy to know that somehow, she'd have help. She believed Jesse.

The plantation was on the banks of the west side of the Mississippi. Emma walked away from the river, into the woods west of the plantation. She stopped briefly and stood in the moonlight. It was a clear night, and the moon was more than half-full, and she could see in the woods enough to travel. She took the scissors out of her bag, and started to cut her hair short, so she could pass as a man. She put the scissors back in the bag and kept walking.

Jesse had told her about the land north and west of the plantation. There wasn't much except for some homesteads and a lot of forest. She would just keep walking. She knew how to navigate by moon, sun and stars, so she knew which direction to go in. For some reason, she was confident—confident that she would be fine and find that strange man.

She traveled relatively quickly for a few weeks and was able to avoid people. She'd had a few close calls but hadn't been discovered. She had traveled a lot at night and found abandoned barns and other places to sleep. Sometimes she'd sleep in a tree.

Today, though, Emma was hungry. She hadn't managed to find much to eat in days. Early on she'd had a lot of luck finding fruit to eat along the way, and she'd caught some fish in the bayous. But for some reason during the last few days she hadn't had much luck finding anything.

She could see in the distance a little cabin surrounded by sugar fields that had just recently been harvested. She was desperate—if she didn't get anything to eat soon, she would starve. She walked slowly and carefully to the cabin and didn't see anyone in evidence. As she came closer, she saw one single creole woman who looked to be pretty old, sitting in a chair several yards away from the cabin, mostly facing away from her. She dropped her bag at the corner of the cabin, right where she could pick it up when she ran out. She walked very quietly and got close to the door of the cabin when the woman got up from her chair, turned and looked right at her and started walking toward her.

"Hungry?" Emma didn't know exactly what to say. She realized she had nothing to lose.

"Yes, mighty hungry."

"I will get you something. You stay here." The woman got up, and walked into the cabin, and came out with a bowl that had rice and red beans. It smelled heavenly to Emma.

"Thank you."

"You are welcome. You should rest here a while. It is safe."

"Safe?"

"Yes. It's safe here. My husband owns this farm, and nobody bothers us. You could stay awhile—help us around the house."

Emma couldn't immediately see why she shouldn't stay a while. They had food, and she did need to rest and get her bearings. She noticed that like many creoles she had met in her life, the woman spoke differently than other people she knew—more like her masters, but differently than that, too.

She wolfed down the beans and rice—before she knew it, the bowl was completely empty. She handed it back to the woman.

"What is your name, girl?" Emma was a little surprised, but she let it go.

"Emma."

"Well, Emma, my name is Delphine. My husband and I were born around here. You have been traveling a while? Where are you from?"

For some reason, Emma told Delphine the whole story—from giving birth to her daughter, to being sold, to escaping during the Union takeover of Baton Rouge.

"That is some story, Emma. Well, it is good that you made it this far without being caught. Get your bag, I'll show you where you can sleep."

She walked to the corner of the cabin and picked up her bag and walked inside the cabin. As her eyes got accustomed to the light inside, she could see the cabin was very well furnished. There were shelves with books, and nice furniture. It was a contrast to the outside of the cabin.

Delphine pointed Emma toward a room in the back with three beds.

"My oldest daughter got married a few months ago and left us. So now there is a bed for you. It's that one in the corner. I'll get you some blankets and sheets."

Delphine and Emma talked while Delphine made the bed.

"You look tired child. Take a nap. I'll wake you when my husband and children get home."

"Thank you, Delphine." Almost before Emma's head hit the pillow, she was deeply asleep.

Outside Natchitoches, Louisiana, December 16, 1862

Emma was sitting in the living room, patching Delphine's dress, when she heard voices outside of the cabin. She wondered what was happening. Of course, she always wondered what was happening and why. Those questions got her into more trouble than they were worth, in general, but she couldn't help it.

Life with Delphine's family had been quiet. She'd been working hard for them—sewing, cooking, doing household chores. She didn't mind—they fed her and took care of her. She was thinking about when she would leave, though. It felt like it was close to time.

The cabin door opened, and Delphine came in.

"Emma, gather up your things." Emma looked up.

"Why, Missus?"

"There's a man here. He's going to take you to Texas."

Delphine knew that she was hoping to go out West to get her freedom. They had talked about it a few times.

"He take me to Texas? Where in Texas?" She was hopeful.

Delphine nodded her head, and said, "You can ask him." Something about her manner didn't sit right with Emma. Something was wrong.

"Who is he Missus?"

"Emma, gather your things—you are going this minute, hear?"

Emma obeyed, and went to the room with her bed, and packed up her small bag. She came back into the living room, but Delphine was gone. She walked outside into the sun. She saw a white man standing next to a wagon. Delphine was nowhere in sight.

"You Emma, eh?" She nodded. "Well, then, c'mon. I don't have all day."

Emma knew this wasn't right. He didn't look like he could be trusted. He didn't look like she'd even like him. She backed away.

"I don't think I wanna to go now."

The man laughed. "You think you have a choice, nigger? Come here and get in this wagon this minute. I paid good money for you, and I don't want to have to whip you, girl."

Emma felt a rush of adrenaline. Delphine had betrayed her! She sold her to someone! She turned and ran as fast as she could.

Before she knew it, she was on the ground, tasting dust, with a heavy weight on her back. It was Delphine.

"Get up Emma."

Delphine got off, and Emma stood up, shakily.

"Why, missus?"

"We needed the money. I'm sorry, Emma. This man will treat you fine."

Emma had no such confidence. She picked up her bag and walked toward the wagon feeling nothing.

Chapter 6

Lena Jameson has been called back to Virginia to take care of the plantation because of the death of her brother and father. After long and careful thought, as well as discussion with Mrs. Jameson, I have decided to accompany her to Virginia.

I believe that this will allow me the safest way to experience as much as I can of life in the South under slavery. Without Lena Jameson's help, it would be impossible. I will continue to be in her employ until we reach Texas. Afterwards, it will be necessary for me to pose as her slave. This provides us both with cover and security. She is more secure because of my presence—she will not be traveling as a woman alone. I will be secure because of the perception of being her slave.

There is danger, however. The primary danger is if we accidentally arrive somewhere where there is military activity. She will be hiring a guide to help us navigate, and I will be using my listening devices to help us as well.

I am aware this is a more risky situation than we had anticipated. Please keep close track of my log frequency. I am confident, however, that we both will be fine.

Attached is my final essay on medical care in San Francisco, and climate data.

San Francisco, CA, January 3, 1863/96 Paqn 743

Jam'elo and Lena were lying in bed, talking. Saturdays were their days to relax together. Lena had insisted on hiring a nanny for the children on Saturdays, since Jam'elo worked so hard most of the week—she hardly got a chance to see him.

"So it appears your President Lincoln has ended slavery?"

"No, not really. I read the proclamation—it only covers Confederate territory."

"I don't understand—why would he do that? Why shouldn't it cover all of the states? On Casiti, the Caraj makes a decision based on consensus, and it covers everyone equally. Your system of states and laws is confusing."

"It confuses me too, Jam'elo. I think that this is mostly a political move—it's not really designed to free many people right now. The newspaper said that only a few slaves in Union-held territory were liberated by the proclamation. I guess it is one step along the way, dear heart."

Jam'elo was quiet for a while as he pondered this. It was so different than what he knew of the process that freed humans from slavery under the Tud'scla. There was conflict, for sure—conflict between those who would end up on Casiti and the others. As Jam'elo thought of the others, he had a question for Lena.

"Do you think many of the freed slaves will choose to stay with their masters?"

She answered, "I imagine some will, yes. Some people don't know any other life. Are you thinking about the Za'aref?"

Jam'elo nodded. He had told Lena about the Za'aref: those who chose to try and stay with the Tud'scla, and eventually were separated from the Casitians. He hoped he would have the chance to learn more about those here who would choose to stay with their masters.

San Francisco, CA, January 10, 1863/101 Paqn 743

Jam'elo and Lena had spent two weeks figuring out how they were going to get to Virginia and preparing for their trip. They had several options of how to get to the Mississippi river but going east from there was going to be difficult. It seemed that the best route was to go through Texas and Louisiana, and cross the Mississippi River at Vicksburg, which was still in the hands of the Confederacy. At some point, perhaps in Texas, they needed to find a guide who knew where the conflicts were and could steer around them. There had even been articles in the San Francisco newspaper that suggested such guides were available. Apparently, there were many who needed to travel that territory, although more were going west than east.

They would travel with Jam'elo posing as an employee, until they passed the Texas border. Jam'elo would then pose as a slave, owned by Lena, traveling back home to Virginia. It was a likely story—many people were traveling back to their homes in the south to either sign up to join the Confederate Army or take care of their property.

Jam'elo had an Indian friend, Ahote, and he was willing to travel with them to New Mexico, where his home was. From there, they would head to Houston, where they hoped to find a guide.

They had explained the whole thing to Clara, who understood, and promised to do her best to pretend. They realized that Robert Jr. didn't really need to pretend—except for physical expressions of affection, his relationship to Jam'elo wouldn't look to an outsider much differently than that of a caretaker. They would just have to be careful around strangers. Jam'elo's friend knew exactly what was going on, so they would not need to pretend around him.

Lena had gone about selling most of what she had. She had said that there was no point in bringing any of the furniture, tools, eating utensils and cooking implements because, as she told it, the plantation was overflowing with those sorts of things. They decided that traveling by covered wagon was the best option—there were many available to be bought, since so many had come West.

"So, we leave this Friday. It seems so soon, Jam'elo."

"We'll be ready. Ahote is ready."

Southern California, February 25, 1863/1 Musb 743

They had been traveling for about 5 days, and were finally headed east, and would pass into the newly created Arizona Territory in a few days. They had stocked up at Lane's Crossing with water and supplies, and Jam'elo was confident that they would have more than enough water to make it to the next source. Ahote had been great company. He was friendly to Lena and loved telling the children stories about his home and his people, and they seemed equally eager to hear them. He didn't seem to think that his relationship with Lena was strange. He told the story of a woman in his tribe who is greatly respected, who came from the "Wasi'chu" as he called them. Jam'elo had asked him what that meant, and he said it was a word from another tribe for the white man and meant "he who takes the fat." Jam'elo wrote a small essay for his log about it.

Jam'elo realized that he really loved to travel. Their trip from Oregon to California had been short and uneventful. This was more interesting. They had stopped in many small towns, and Jam'elo had been keenly observing the differences of people in the places that they traveled on their way.

Jam'elo was taking his turn driving the wagon. This time, Clara was on the horse with Lena, and Robert Jr. was on the horse with Ahote. Jam'elo didn't much like the wagon. Actually, none of them did—it was a very rough ride. Ahead of them on the trail, they could see dust, and it looked like a wagon train of some sort was heading toward them. They had met dozens of people leaving the conflict in the South to settle in the West.

"Lena, see that wagon train? Just in case, I want Clara and Robert in the wagon."

"That is a very good idea, Jam'elo." First, Lena came along side of the wagon, and Jam'elo helped Clara off the horse, and into the wagon. Then Ahote picked Robert up, and handed him to Jam'elo, who put him in the back of the wagon as well.

"Clara, take care of your brother, and both of you need to keep very quiet, OK? We don't know who these people are."

"OK Jameelo." Clara held Robert Jr., and Jam'elo closed the front flap of the wagon.

As the lead wagon in the train got closer to them, it slowed down, and did not move from the center of the trail. Clearly, Jam'elo thought, these folks wanted something. He saw Lena kick her horse and move forward. The forward wagon and Jam'elo drew close to each other. Jam'elo could see that the man driving the wagon looked to be in bad shape.

Jam'elo could hear Lena say, "Hello there. Where are you heading?"

"We got family in San Bernadino. We're joining them."

"Where did you come from?"

"We left Alabama. Didn't want to fight in no stupid war. Who are you?"

"I can understand that. My name is Lena Jameson."

"Where are you headed?"

"We're headed to Texas."

"Why?"

"Family."

"Who are those people?" The man thrust his chin toward Jam'elo and Ahote.

"These are Jam'elo and Ahote, and they are in my employ. Is there anything you need?"

The man looked at them suspiciously, and Jam'elo saw several men on horseback that were jittery. One started to move his hand toward a weapon.

Jam'elo said, loudly, "Sir, you don't look so good, sir. Do you need medicine? I can help."

"You can help? What kind of medicine do you have? A lot of us are sick, and some have died on the way."

"Yes, I can help. I can treat you and your people, sir."

"Why should I believe you?"

Jam'elo answered, "Sir, why would I offer if it weren't true?"

"My wife is in the back of this here wagon, and she's dying."

Jam'elo turned and opened the flap to the back of the wagon slightly.

He whispered to Clara, "Hand me that bag, Clara dear." She picked up the bag with his medical kit and handed it to him. He jumped off and walked toward the other wagon.

"Let me see her, sir. I can help, I promise. I can help anyone who needs it."

The man grunted, and got off the wagon, and walked to the back, and climbed in. Jam'elo followed. It took him a moment to adjust to the dim light inside the wagon. He could see the woman lying there in a nest of dirty, smelly blankets. She was feverish and delirious. She looked to him to have agent 19, but he needed to be sure. He took a swab from her mouth, and placed it in his device, which he held in his hands, invisible to the man. Yes, agent 19 it was. He took out the broad-spectrum antibacterial agent he knew would eliminate agent 19, and added a few drops of something to ease her symptoms. He placed three drops on her tongue. She would be better in less than an hour.

"I've given her this tincture. I need to come back and have a look at her in an hour or so, and probably give her some more. She should get better fairly quickly though… sir." He realized his habit of saying "sir" and "ma'am" was not quite perfectly honed.

"We're going to camp here, and you will too. We'll see if this works. You'll be sorry if it doesn't." Jam'elo knew that was an open threat, but it didn't matter. She would be up and walking by the time they finished setting camp.

He left the wagon and walked back toward Lena and Ahote.

"They want us to camp here. He threatened me if his wife doesn't get well."

"Lucky for us you are a miracle worker. How strong?"

"She'll be fine in an hour." Lena raised her eyebrows.

"That strong?"

"I get the impression that if we don't do something miraculous, they are likely to get ornery."

She nodded. "Agreed."

They had agreed that Clara and Robert Jr. would remain hidden, and sleep in the wagon. Junior was sleeping anyway, and Jam'elo quietly read Clara a story inside the wagon while Ahote and Lena made a fire and cooked dinner.

As he was finishing the story, he heard a man's voice say, "We need him to give others in our group that medicine, please." He kissed Clara good night and got out of the wagon with his bag on his shoulder.

"Sir, show me to them."

Jam'elo spent the next couple of hours treating about ten people in their party who were sick, including the man driving the lead wagon, who had never offered his name. None of them had offered their names. The next morning, Jam'elo was awoken by the sound of wagons passing by. He looked at Lena, who was sleeping by his side, but hidden from view.

She said, "They didn't even thank us."

Jam'elo smiled. "Yes they did. They left us alone."

Jam'elo could see the pueblo in the distance, with the collection of houses made from materials that Ahote had said was something called "adobe," a mixture of sand, clay, water and straw. As they rode into the pueblo, Jam'elo thought that these dwellings were the closest he had seen so far to those on Casiti.

"Ahote, these houses look something like the ones we make back home."

Ahote turned toward Jam'elo and smiled. "They are very suited to this climate. I miss how they feel when I am away."

People began to come out of their houses to watch them, and at one point a group of children ran up to the wagon, shouting and playing. Clara and Robert Jr. wanted to get down from the wagon and be with the children. Ahote assured Lena they would be fine.

An older woman walked toward them, and Ahote got down from his horse and ran to embrace her. Everyone stopped where they were.

Ahote said, "Jam'elo, Lena, this is Kasa, my mother. She doesn't understand English—she speaks our native tongue, and Spanish."

Lena walked up to Kasa and said, "Hola Kasa, es muy agradable conocer a la madre de un hijo tan noble."

Kasa smiled, and said, "El placer es mío. Usted es bienvenida aquí."

Lena turned to Jam'elo. "I said, 'Hello Kasa, it is nice to meet the mother of such a noble son.' She replied, 'The pleasure is mine. You are welcome here.'"

Jam'elo knew that Lena was fluent in several languages. He didn't realize Spanish was one of them. He chuckled to himself—she surprised him all the time.

They followed Ahote and Kasa to the collection of dwellings occupied by Ahote's family. Other family members greeted Ahote with gusto, and were warm and welcoming to Jam'elo, Lena and the children.

Ahote said to them, "They are planning a feast to celebrate my return, and to honor you as our guests."

Jam'elo was looking forward to some rest and relaxation for a few days. He knew the trip onward would be brutal.

Eastern Texas, March, 1863

Emma really felt the third stroke. The first two had been bad enough, but with the third, it was like someone had lit her back on fire. Somehow, in all her life, she had avoided the lash. Mostly because even though she asked a lot of questions, she always did as she was told. But these masters didn't like any of her questions—they just wanted her be completely silent.

With the fourth stroke, her back was more than just on fire—it felt as though the whip was ripping through her flesh, and she was being flayed. On the fifth stroke, she felt the warmth of her bladder emptying, and then she passed out.

She woke up still attached to the whipping post. Her wrists and arms were sore, and her back felt like there were still smoldering coals attached to them.

"You woke up, finally." She heard her mistress, then felt her warm breath on her cheek, and smelled the tobacco on her breath.

"What're we gonna do wit' you Emma? You talk too much."

Emma was silent. Then, she could feel the ropes being untied, but before she could support herself, she crumpled to the ground.

"Get up!" She struggled to get on her hands and knees from being in a heap on the ground. Then she struggled to stand. Finally, she stood, wobbling.

"Go clean yourself up, you made a mess. Then finish that woodpile! And I don't want to hear one word from you!"

She walked slowly to the back of their house, which had a well with water that the slaves used. Henry, one of the field hands, took her arm over his shoulder, and helped her into a bench.

"Just a minute. I'ma go get my Margerie to hep you clean up."

Emma could only nod. The next hour was a blur—Margarie found her a new shift, and washed her up, and they both helped her back to her bed. She protested mildly, since she was supposed to finish the woodpile.

Henry said, "Girl, you ain't gonna do nothing until tomorrow. You need to heal. I'll handle the wood pile."

Once in her bed, she fell asleep instantly.

After that day, some weeks would go by without a lashing, but most didn't. Tonight, Emma tossed and turned in her uncomfortable cot, her back hurting from yesterday's beating, and she finally gave up. She swung her legs over the side of the cot and sat upright. Her missus had refused to feed her today, and Emma was famished

At first, the beatings started because she asked too many questions. She always did as she was told, but she always wondered why, and her masters asked her to do some things that didn't make a lot of sense to her. And she just wanted to learn. There were things they did differently, and ways they lived differently, and she wanted to know why.

She stopped asking the questions aloud, even though they still went on in her head. But the beatings continued, and she finally realized that they did it just because they could. At first, it made her mad, but then that just made things worse. After a while, she just became resigned to it, but the anger simmered under the surface.

Her empty stomach was aching, and she needed to get some food. She looked in the dark for her shoes, put them on, put a heavy shirt over her dress, and walked out of the cabin to sneak into the house kitchen, where all of the food was kept.

She very quietly made her way across the small yard between the cabin where she and the other slaves slept, and the house where her master and missus lived. She noticed that the clotheslines still had yesterday's laundry on it. It was quiet, and there were no lamps lit in the house that she could see. She tip-toed onto the back porch, turned the knob on the kitchen door very, very slowly, and walked into the kitchen. She remembered to leave the door wide open in case she needed to run for it.

As she made her way into the dark kitchen toward where she knew the panty was, she banged into a large barrel, which tipped over, spilled and splashed something liquid all over the kitchen floor. She was paralyzed with fear. She finally got her wits about her, but by then the liquid was quickly spreading. It smelled like kerosene. She had no idea what to do—there was going to be no way to clean it up. She then heard footsteps in the room next to the kitchen, and she saw her master come into the kitchen, carrying a lamp.

He stepped into the kitchen, and she heard him say, "What's going on he..."

He slipped on the floor and fell, dropping the lamp. The lamp ignited the kerosene, setting her master on fire, and everything else, too. Emma fled the kitchen, hearing her master's screams. She had the presence of mind, somehow, to grab some of her master's clothes from the clothesline, and then she ran into the fields.

She kept running through the fields until she was out of breath. She looked back at the house, which was by now completely engulfed in flames. She realized she needed to keep moving. She looked up at the sky, figured out the right direction, and then resumed running, and ran through the fields into the forest. She had probably managed to kill her master at least, and with the speed the fire spread, she probably also killed missus, too. It was an accident, but somehow, she didn't care.

She ran through the woods for as long as she could, and then stopped to rest. She couldn't see the flames anymore—she had probably run a couple of miles. She took the small knife she always carried out of the pocket of her dress and started to chop off her hair as best she could. She then took off the dress, and put on her master's shirt, pants, and put her heavy shirt over that, and then the jacket. They were a little large but fit her well enough. She then ripped up the dress and dropped it on the ground.

She got up to walk—she realized that she should walk as far as she could during the night, then find somewhere to hide as it got light out. It was a clear night, and she could see some of the stars, enough to know which direction to keep moving. The moon was still pretty new and wouldn't rise until close to the morning.

As the eastern sky behind her began to tinge with yellow, she looked ahead and saw a small farmstead. She would have to avoid it. She didn't know how long she could go without finding something to eat, but she thought she'd deal with that later.

As she wound around the farmstead, she found a small river, and realized that she was thirsty. She drank deeply of it. It stank a little, but she couldn't worry about that now. She kept walking, and found a small group of boulders, and she nestled in between them, and slept.

She was awoken by the voice of a boy. "Look, Mattie—we got a nigger here!"

Her eyes popped open, and she saw three blond-haired boys looking at her. One of them ran away—she imagined to get an adult. One of them had a stick, which he started to poke at her. She decided she needed to get away from the boys, and out of the area. She got up and ran in the opposite direction from where the boys were. She didn't hear them follow. She kept running, toward the setting sun. She slowed down after a while and kept walking well into the night.

The forest was giving way to open land, and she stopped briefly when she got severe pains in her stomach. She thought they might be hunger pains, but all of a sudden she needed to relieve herself, and her bowels were liquid. She realized then she was sick. She decided to take a rest in a small copse of trees.

When it became light, she awoke and was delirious. All she felt knew was a need to push on. She didn't know the right direction to walk in, so she just walked in the direction she assumed was away from where she had been.

At one point, she looked down at her feet to see that the meadow that she had been walking on changed to a smooth mud texture. She couldn't for the life of her figure out what was going on, and the world started spinning around. She fell and lay there for a while.

The last thing she remembered was hearing a man's voice saying, "I got me a lost nigger. Wonder how much he'll fetch?"

Dallas, Texas, April 25, 1863

Jam'elo felt like the dust was caked to his skin by sweat. He could hardly stand his own odor, and he wanted a bath so badly he could taste it, but he imagined that a bath was unlikely for him for the foreseeable future. His best bet was to find a river to swim in. They were on the road into Dallas, and they had been traveling for a while, after leaving Ahote behind with his family at Taos Pueblo, in New Mexico. Ahote's family had been so generous, and had hosted them for a few days, letting them rest and get their bearings. He liked spending time among the Indians—he felt like he understood them better than just about anyone else he had come across. Except Lena, of course.

Now that they were in Texas, Jam'elo was no longer Lena's employee. He was Lena's slave. He noticed that she was taking it very seriously. He didn't even mind calling her or Clara "mistress," or Robert Jr. "master." Robert Jr. seemed to be enjoying bossing Jam'elo around, and Lena had almost made the mistake of chastising him about it in public.

In fact, he realized that although it was surprisingly possible for him to act correctly in public, he could not take the whole thing very seriously. There was one time when he broke out in laughter, and the look that Lena gave him was enough to snap him out of it.

Jam'elo was driving the wagon somewhat absentmindedly as they neared the city. Just ahead of him he could see a wagon with a crumpled form in the back, in chains. His anger flared. The man inside the wagon looked injured or sick. Jam'elo motioned to Lena. She drew closer to the wagon. He pointed.

"Yes, Jam'elo I see that."

"We need to help. He looks sick."

"Jam'elo…"

"We need to help him, Lena!"

She nodded, and kicked her heels gently, and her horse sped up. She caught up with the wagon ahead, and began to talk with the driver. Jam'elo could not hear what was said, but after several minutes, the wagon slowed, and Lena motioned to Jam'elo. He grabbed his medical kit, and got off their wagon, and went to treat the man in the back of the other wagon. As he began to work, he overheard Lena and the man talking.

"Well, you sure have helped me ma'am. Two hundred dollars seems like more than a fair price for this one. He's bound to die soon, and I know I won't find the bounty in time."

"He'll be fine—I have faith in my man here. He knows how to treat his people. Do you have the lock for those chains?"

"Ma'am, you don't want to unchain him. He's a runaway."

"He's not going anywhere anytime soon—he's very sick."

Jam'elo set to work on the man. He could see it was a case of agent 31. Mostly the problem here was with massive dehydration. Jam'elo went back into their wagon, and grabbed the gallon jug of treated water, and filled his canteen up with it. He had given the man some of the antibiotic solution that would eliminate the factor. He now had to get the man to start drinking water.

He decided to check for any other injuries for good measure. He looked up, and saw that the driver was still facing away, and busily talking with Lena. He took out his medical imager, and quickly did a check all over his body. What he found surprised him—this wasn't a man, but a woman who was trying to pass as a man. Jam'elo realized that the driver had no idea. He would tell Lena later.

There weren't any other major injuries, except for some nasty festering wounds on her back, but he could deal with those later. He put the imager away and stepped out of the wagon.

"Mistress, he'll be fine in a little bit."

"Thank you, Jam'elo. We need to put him in our wagon."

The driver stepped down into the well of the wagon and unlocked the chains around the woman. Jam'elo picked her up, and took her to the back of their wagon, where Clara and Robert Jr. were sitting.

"Little one, do me a favor. When she wakes up, ask her to drink from this canteen? Alright?"

"Alright Jam'elo. Who is she? She looks like a man."

"She's with us now, Clara. I'm sure we'll find out more later, little one."

Jam'elo climbed to the front of the wagon and sat in the driver's seat. Lena had paid the man out of their cash supply, and he had moved on.

Jam'elo said, "I didn't quite expect you to buy her."

"Her?"

"Yes, she is a woman."

"He didn't know that." She jutted her chin out toward the man who was at an increasing distance ahead of them.

"I could tell from the way he talked that purchasing her was going to be the only way we could help her. He wouldn't have understood anything else, and he wasn't going to let her go."

"Well, anyway, she will be fine. What are we going to do with her now that you own her?"

"I don't know, Jam'elo. You got me into this!"

"I guess I did, didn't I?"

They rode in silence until they reached the center of town, where Lena found the local hotel. They stopped in front, and Lena went in, and returned with the proprietress. She was pointing around the back, and he suspected that was where he was going to stay. In a barn, likely. He didn't really mind, except that he wasn't going to get a bath.

Lena walked up to him stiffly. "Jam'elo, behind this building and down that alley are the stables for the hotel. Bring the wagon and the horses there, and her man will show you where the stalls are. He will also show you where you can park the wagon. Mrs. Wilson says he also knows where you can sleep and get something to eat."

"Yes mistress. Let me help you with the things you and the children need."

He could tell that this was wearing on her, allowing him to do everything. He could tell she hated it. And his heart ached for her. They hadn't had a chance to be alone together in days, and he hoped they could arrange that sometime soon, but he had no idea when that would be. He finished unpacking the wagon for her and the children, and went to the back of the hotel, where he was met by a man who introduced himself as "Bernard."

"Where you comin' from?" Jam'elo knew better than to immediately trust him. They had agreed that they would say they were from Houston and were traveling back to Virginia.

Bernard asked, "You goin' all de way to 'ginny?"

Jam'elo answered, "Yes, that's where the plantation is."

Bernard peered at Jam'elo. "You sure talk strange. And you look strange—you don't look right to be no slave."

"Look, I'm hungry and tired, and I have a sick man I need to take care of. Can you tell me where to put these horses and wagon, and show me where to get some food, and where my friend and I can sleep?"

"Well, these here stalls are empty. There's grain in that barrel over there. You can park the wagon on the side of the stable." He then pointed to a small corner of the stable. "You two can sleep over 'dere. I bring you both some food."

"Thank you. We only need food for me—he's not ready to eat yet." Jam'elo parked the wagon and got in to look on the new member of their company. She was awake and staring at him.

"Have you been drinking the water like Clara told you to?"

"Clara, that her name?"

"Yes."

"Yes, I been drinkin'. Who you?"

"My name is Jam'elo. Look, we should get you out of this wagon—there's a place for you to sleep in the barn. And I have to take a look at those injuries on your back."

She slowly crawled toward the back of the wagon and sat at the edge with her legs dangling down. Jam'elo stood beside her and put his arm under hers and helped her down. Jam'elo kept propping her up as they walked to the barn, and when they got to the corner, he helped her down onto the straw.

"Let me go get the jug and canteen. You are badly dehydrated, and you need to drink a lot of water."

"Dehydra...?"

"You need water."

She nodded, slowly. Jam'elo went to get his kit, and the water, and put them in the barn next to her. He handed the canteen to her.

"Drink more of this, now."

She nodded, and tipped the canteen to her lips, and drank several gulps. Jam'elo asked her to lift up her shirt so he could see the wounds on her back. She resisted, but then finally agreed. He put some bandages on the wounds soaked with a solution of nanoparticles that would heal the wounds completely. When he was done, she curled into a ball, and fell asleep.

Jam'elo set about getting the horses fed and brushed down. Just as he was finished, Bernard came up to him with a bowl and a spoon.

Bernard said, "Here some food."

Jam'elo answered, "Thank you."

Jam'elo took his bag and some blankets from the wagon and sat down in the stall to eat. There was a square of corn bread, which was dry, but good, and some stew with unidentifiable meat. When he finished eating, he took some prophylactic antibacterial, just in case.

He looked over at his charge, who was awake and watching him.

Jam'elo asked, "What's your name?"

She said, "Edward."

Jam'elo decided to go along for now. "Hello, Edward."

"Where am I?"

"Dallas, Texas."

"Why ain't I in chains no mo'?"

"Your new owner doesn't believe in them."

"I got a new Massa?"

"Well, not really. It's hard to explain."

She peered at him. "You ain't no slave, are you?"

He put a finger to his lips. "Shhhh. I'm supposed to be, but you are right, I'm not."

She kept peering at him in a way he found uncomfortable.

"You gonna hep me, ain't ye?"

"I already did, some, and I guess I'll help you more. There is a lot to explain. But you will be fine."

"I'm free?"

"Um, well, look, let's wait a bit, alright? We have to figure all of that out."

She shook her head, took more from the canteen, and curled up and fell asleep. Jam'elo thought it would be good for him to follow suit. He curled up in the other corner on the blankets.

He was woken up by someone nudging his leg.

"Time to get up."

At first, he didn't know where he was, but then remembered. He slowly got up and brushed himself off. He looked over to see his charge, who was awake, and drinking from the canteen.

Bernard was looking at him. "Your mistress told me to get ya. She wants ta see you in her room 'mmediately, she says. Sound like you in *big* trouble."

Jam'elo did his best to hide his elation. How logical of Lena—to pretend she needed to see him for disciplinary reasons.

"I'll be right back, Edward."

He got up, and Bernard guided him to the back door of the hotel. Another man inside showed him to Lena's room. He hurried, and he knew that these men would simply think that he was worried.

The second man was behind him as he knocked on the door. Lena answered and had a very stern look on her face. It was all he could do not to smile.

Jam'elo said seriously, "You wanted me, Mistress?"

"Yes, Jam'elo. I am very upset. Come in." She looked toward the other man and said, "Thank you." He nodded and left.

As Jam'elo walked into the room and closed the door, Lena curled up her nose. "You stink, dear one. I wish I could draw you a bath."

He smiled. "So do I."

His smell didn't stop her from kissing him fiercely. "I miss you." She was crying. "I don't know if I can do this, Jam'elo."

"We can do it. We're together, my love." She was still crying when she pulled apart from him.

"I found a guide. His name is Martin. He has contacts in the Confederate Army and has successfully guided people all the way to North Carolina and Virginia. Honestly, I don't like him, but he comes well recommended."

"When do we leave?"

"He is willing to leave tomorrow. He says he can get us to Richmond in 60 days. I need to order some provisions today, which, of course, you need to go pick up. And I guess now you have help? How is she doing?"

"She's doing fine. Confused, but fine."

"She'll probably stay confused for a while, I suspect. Anyway, I'm also going to post a letter to my mother letting her know about when to expect us."

She looked at him with her gentleness, and he wished that they could have more time together alone.

She said, "I'll try to arrange a bath or something for you. I know you would appreciate that." He smiled.

She sighed, smiled at him, and then threw him a kiss. She then started shouting. "I never, ever want you to do that again, do you hear me?" She opened the door.

"Yes, Mistress, never again."

She kept shouting. "Now get downstairs and take care of the horses. I'll send you to the store when I've ordered the provisions."

"Yes'm." He hazarded a last smile, and then walked down the hall with his head hanging.

Eastern Texas, April 26, 1863

Emma awoke confused. She wasn't in her cot, and she couldn't figure out why everything smelled like a barn. She looked around and remembered yesterday. One minute she had been captured and chained in a wagon, and the next being given medicine and water by a strange man. She didn't feel like she could trust this, or him yet—it was all too new, too unexpected.

Yesterday, in her delirium, she dreamt about being taken and hanged for killing her masters. She also dreamt about being sold and dreamt about seeing her daughter being whipped. She could hardly believe how much her fortunes had changed in one day.

She sat up and watched the strange man sleep. He wasn't a white man, yet he didn't look like her, or any other mulatto or quadroon she'd ever seen. She remembered how good his teeth looked, and how he talked. She wondered who he was, and where he came from.

She looked down and saw the canteen and remembered that he'd demanded that she drink from it. She certainly was thirsty, and getting hungry, too. Her back didn't hurt at all anymore, and she felt fine— better than she had felt in a long time.

She didn't know what was next, and where they were going. She wondered whether or not he was the man Jesse told her about. She'd wait and see.

Eastern Texas, May 1, 1863

Jam'elo looked at Martin. He had recognized Martin immediately as the man whose friend he had saved years ago on the Oregon trail, but he could tell that Martin didn't remember him. He figured it was context—it seemed likely that Martin would remember him if he was traveling as a doctor. But of course, that would be impossible here. He saw that Martin had lost an arm, and in passing, Jam'elo had heard him tell Lena he had been a Confederate soldier in the war.

He could tell that Martin was showing a particular kind of behavior toward Lena—behavior Jam'elo had learned signaled Martin's interest in her. He hoped that wouldn't become a problem later. Of course, Jam'elo knew that Lena would be considered a prime catch—the widower daughter of a rich landowner of Richmond.

Martin had also taken to ordering Jam'elo and "Edward" about, until Lena had let him know that they were only hers to command. Jam'elo noticed that Martin paid more attention to Jam'elo after that. He wasn't quite sure why, but he wondered whether Lena's behavior toward Jam'elo wasn't quite what it should be.

Jam'elo always drove the wagon, with "Edward" beside him. For a while, his posterior was really feeling it, but he had gotten used to it. Clara was now riding her own horse that Lena had bought before they left Dallas. Robert Jr. was still in the wagon mostly, but sometimes he rode with his mother. They had given Jam'elo's horse to Ahote's family in New Mexico—it was a large, beautiful, strong mare, was too big for Clara, and wasn't suited to pulling a wagon. As a slave, Jam'elo wouldn't look right riding it.

"Edward" had been no more forthcoming to either him or Lena over the past few days. She wasn't unfriendly, but she seemed to be very careful. Jam'elo couldn't quite understand why.

They rode mostly in silence. Martin would sometimes regale them with stories of the road, and the times he had come close to one battle or another. Jam'elo noticed that Martin never talked about the battle in which he had lost his arm, or much about his past. Sometimes, when Martin rode up ahead out of earshot, Jam'elo and Lena would talk. Those were cherished moments. And they learned they could be dangerous. One day, Martin had ridden up ahead, ostensibly to scout out an easier way around a washed-out road.

Lena sidled up to the wagon and reached her hand out.

Jam'elo reached out and touched her hand, and said, "Hey love, how are you? I know how hard this is on you. I think it's harder on you than it is on me."

"It's alright, dear heart. I'm not worried about your safety anymore—you were right, this was the right idea. But it is so hard to remember to treat you badly. I never did so well at that when I was at home in Virginia—I can't imagine that I'm doing such a good job of it now."

Jam'elo laughed. "You are not treating me badly. I think Martin notices."

"Yes, I don't trust him."

"He likes you."

She made a face. "Ugh."

"I just noticed it…"

"I know, I know. I'm just avoiding facing the reality of it."

All of a sudden, Jam'elo heard a noise in the brush near them, and he put his finger over his lips. The noise kept happening, and then Martin burst out of the brush right next to them.

"I found the way around. It's an old track, probably for cattle. You will have to pull the wagon through it with only one horse; I don't think it's wide enough for both horses." He was looking at Jam'elo.

Jam'elo looked at Lena, who said, "Jam'elo, can you unhitch the horses, and follow Martin's lead?"

"Yes ma'am."

A few days later, "Edward" said to Jam'elo, "Emma, my name is Emma."

Jam'elo smiled. "Thank you for telling me, Emma."

He was glad that she was opening up to him. Emma and Jam'elo were talking as they drove the wagon. Lena and Clara were just ahead of them, and Martin was far up ahead scouting out the road.

Emma said, "I didn't know if I could trust you."

He nodded. "I understand."

"You're different."

Jam'elo nodded. "I'm from very far away."

"Clara done tol' me yesterday, you from the sky. Jesse tol' me I fine you."

"Jesse?"

"Jesse my friend, back at the plantation, before I lef'. He blind, but he have the sight, ya know?"

117

Jam'elo didn't know. "The sight?"

"He can see the future."

Jam'elo nodded. "I see." Jam'elo knew that it was a known trait that a few humans had, to see things others couldn't.

"So, he saw you meeting me?"

"Yessir, he did. What we gonna do when we get back to 'ginny?"

Jam'elo chuckled. "Emma, I'm just trying hard to get us there. I don't exactly know what we'll do once we arrive, except that we'll live on Lena's plantation for a while."

"We be free?"

Jam'elo nodded. "Yes, Emma, we'll be free."

Eastern Mississippi, May 7, 1863

They had set up camp, Emma was getting dinner ready, and Jam'elo was out getting wood. Lena was sitting with Clara and Robert Jr., talking with them while she mended a dress. Martin was sitting across from her, staring at her in a way that made her nervous.

"Mother, when are we going to get to Virginia?"

"In about two months, Clara."

"That's forever. I'm tired of this trip!"

Lena chuckled. "Clara, dear, I'm more tired of this trip than you are!"

Clara started to say something, then looked over at Martin, and stopped. Lena suspected it was a question about Jam'elo. Clara was getting very wise, and Lena was proud of her.

"I imagine you have many people waiting for you at the end of this trip, Mrs. Jameson." Martin said that statement in a way that was both dripping with envy, as well as invasive of her privacy. It rankled. She saw him take a swig from his flask. She wondered how deep into his cups he was.

She nodded quickly and slightly, hoping he wasn't interested in pursuing the question more.

"Well, there is much I can offer you in Virginia, ma'am. I think you'd rather like me."

He had been making his interest in her obvious over the past few days, and she had been trying to do her best to ignore it. She was afraid of the moment when she would have to tell him she was not interested. She was putting that off as long as she could, because she suspected that he would take it badly, and she would regret it later.

He said, "Don't you like me?"

She was about to open her mouth, and Jam'elo came out of the woods.

Jam'elo said, "I got a nice amount of wood here—we should be set for a couple of days."

Lena exhaled. "Thank you, Jam'elo. Can you help Emma with the rest of dinner?" Lena used that moment to get up and go to the wagon.

After dinner, Martin went to the other side of the wagon, and fell into his bedroll. Lena had noticed that he had been drinking steadily all evening. She imagined he would be deeply asleep in his drunken stupor.

Lena put the children to bed in the wagon and sat with Emma and Jam'elo. Lena was surprised at the topic they were discussing.

Jam'elo said, "You said you know the constellation Orion."

Emma nodded. "Dat my favorite."

"Why?"

"I imagine a strong man—a man so strong nobody can make him a slave."

"Is that how strong you want to be?"

Emma nodded.

Jam'elo smiled. "So my planet moves around a star in Orion just like the Earth goes around the sun. My planet is very far away."

"How far?"

"Can you imagine how far it is between here and the sun?"

"It 90 million miles—I read dat in a book I had. But figurin' a million—that's way far."

"Well, where I come from is 50 million times the distance between here and the sun."

Emma whistled. "I can't figure dat—dat's really, really far!"

"I can teach you, if you want to learn."

Emma nodded vigorously. "Yes, please, teach me Jameelo!"

Outside Raleigh, North Carolina, June 15, 1863

Martin sat on his horse, staring at Jameelo. He had finally put all of the pieces together. Something about him and his name had always seemed familiar, but he never could remember what it was. Something about Mrs. Jameson's family and that man had always seemed, well, wrong, somehow. Mrs. Jameson seemed to have to work hard to figure out how to tell Jameelo what to do, and the children seemed to like Jameelo too much. At times when they thought he wasn't around, they would talk like he knew no slave and master talked.

Last week, Lena had gotten terrible diarrhea, and Martin watched as Jameelo treated her, and she got better far faster than she should have. Just like Edwin had. That was when he remembered Jameelo.

He had agreed to take them all the way back to Virginia because he wanted to go home, finally. He would be returning with more money than he had when he was there last time. As they traveled, he had begun to spin the idea of courting Lena. Marrying her could make his dreams of being a Southern Gentleman come true. But she had made it clear to him that she wasn't interested, and now he knew: Jameelo was who she loved.

He turned and spit. A plan was beginning to form in his head, one that would help him get started in Virginia. A mulatto as healthy and strong as Jam'elo would fetch a very high price. It was true, Lena would never talk to him again after this, but it didn't matter to him.

Chapter 7

Expedition Log 743.5.22 Student: Jam'elo z Kadarin, 88 Musb

We are now only a few days away from Richmond, Virginia, and Lena Jameson's family plantation. On the whole, it has been an uneventful trip. Posing as her slave has allowed us both to travel safely through the southern part of this continent. I have experienced some of what the slaves here must experience, but it of course has been tempered by the fact that it is pretend, and I am actually free.

On the other hand, I also know that this freedom is in a sense limited. I can leave this planet. I can travel to a place outside of this area with Lena and be free again, but I am truly not free within this area. If Lena and I were to separate, I would quickly be captured and likely sold.

We have gained a new traveler. Her name is Emma, and she was a slave, until Lena bought her, and then officially freed her. She will travel back with us to Virginia. She is smart and insatiably curious. I've begun to teach her math, physics, and astronomy, and she has progressed very rapidly. I fear for her safety and life in Virginia.

I do look forward to ending this part of the travel which has been mostly uncomfortable.

Attached are climate data. I will return to writing the list of planned essays when we reach Richmond.

Petersburg, Virginia, June 30, 1863

Lena said, "Where is he?"

Jam'elo could see that Lena was worried. Martin had left only the vaguest message behind with Jam'elo and Emma, while Lena had been taking care of some business in Petersburg, their last stop before going to on to Richmond.

Jam'elo answered, "He said he was meeting some general or another to find out the best way from here up to Richmond."

"Last I heard, there wasn't any fighting anywhere along this way. The fighting is all up north of Richmond."

"I know, that's what I understand as well. It's a little strange for him to abandon us now, don't you think? We can make it ourselves up to Richmond, and he hasn't gotten the balance of his payment for being our guide. He is about 12 hours overdue."

"Well, I say we wait until morning, and if he hasn't shown up, we'll leave without him."

Jam'elo nodded. He and Lena were sitting in a stall in the barn with the horses. Emma was taking care of Clara and Robert Jr. The town they were staying in was tiny, and the inn in which Lena had gotten a room was not well taken care of. The barn was deserted, so they could safely talk there. They spent a little time holding each other.

"Well, when we make it to my plantation, we can arrange time alone."

"Your mother will allow this?"

"She won't know; I'll make sure of that. I'll place you in the house, where at least you'll have a comfortable place to stay. But I've decided that I am going to free all of the slaves anyway."

"I remember when the Emancipation Proclamation was signed, you said that if you were home, you would have freed all of the slaves that minute."

"Jam'elo, now that you have been a slave, what do you think?"

"Well, I haven't *really* been a slave, of course. I have learned a lot from Emma, though, and I will have to explain to Re'ten that we both were wrong, and why."

"What do you mean?"

"Re'ten and I had a discussion once. He insisted that the experience of people who are enslaved by an alien race must be qualitatively worse than the experience of those enslaved by other human beings. I disagreed and thought that they would be exactly the same. We both were wrong. I'm beginning to believe that effects of this kind of slavery is worse, I think *because* those who keep slaves are also humans. The keepers and the kept are intertwined in ways that would not happen if

122

the species were different, and there is no chance of human solidarity against an alien enemy."

Lena looked thoughtful. "I have to introduce you to someone when we get back to Richmond."

"Who?"

"A free Negro man I knew. He has, in his own quiet way, been trying to form human solidarity for his whole life."

"Has it worked?"

She shook her head. "No. I'm not sure it will ever work."

After a while, she left to go back to her room, and Jam'elo settled into his bed in the stable. Emma returned, and they talked for a time. She was telling him more and more of her story. It was most illuminating for Jam'elo. He learned things he could not quite believe.

They were woken up by Martin. "Get up, Jameelo, Edward. We're leaving."

Jam'elo was a little bleary from being asleep, but he thought Martin's attitude was different. He didn't have time to wonder. They hitched the horses to the wagon, brought it out front, and loaded it up. He said hello to Robert Jr. who looked quite bothered by being awake and picked him up to placed him in the wagon. Martin was looking restless on his horse.

Lena came out of the front of the inn. "Where were you, Martin? We expected you yesterday."

"I was busy. I have the route to Richmond. We will be at your plantation in 2 days.

"Martin, I am paying you to be our guide, not to disappear without explanation."

"I'm sorry. Look, I'm here now. Can we go?" He seemed impatient to Jam'elo. Something was wrong, but Jam'elo could not put his finger on it.

Outside of Richmond, July 2, 1863/92 Musb 743

Jam'elo wasn't really paying attention, which was probably his downfall. Martin had asked Lena if it were OK if Jam'elo got on a horse and went up ahead to scout out the road. Martin said he was concerned that last night's rain may have washed part of it out. Lena knew that Jam'elo missed riding, and any opportunity was welcome. He hadn't had one in weeks. Martin said he hadn't been feeling so well and needed to go slowly. Emma took the reins of the wagon, and Jam'elo happily got on Clara's horse, and rode up ahead to look at the road.

Jam'elo rode about a mile ahead, and the road looked fine to him, and as he crested a hill, he could see Richmond in the distance. There was no trouble, or washout on the road. Jam'elo was a bit puzzled and turned his horse around. Out of the woods came three men on horseback. One of them had a rifle pointed toward him.

"Get off that horse." Jam'elo complied. Two men got off their horses.

One of the men carried what looked to Jam'elo to be shackles. Jam'elo had about three seconds. He knew that Lena would understand, although he felt the sadness of it. It was, perhaps, that hesitation that made the difference. He reached into his pocket, and one of the men grabbed his arm, and pulled out the hand that clasped his emergency communicator. They grabbed it before he had had a chance to activate it.

"What the hell is that thing?" the man who was still on the horse exclaimed. "Give that to me."

"Martin said that this man wasn't what he or his mistress said he was. But it don't matter. He's healthy. He'll fetch a nice price."

They shackled him, then threw him over his horse. He didn't know what he could do to get out of this situation. His last log entry was sent six Earth days ago. They would be expecting another entry today. In three days, when they had not received a message from him, they would know he was in trouble, and start doing what they could to rescue him. And he knew they would rescue him.

He started to cry. He could not imagine a way he would be able to see Lena again.

Outside of Richmond, July 2, 1863

"Martin, how could he just disappear? The horse is gone, too." Martin smiled. A kind of smile Lena wanted to wipe off of his face.

"How do I know? He must have escaped."

"Martin, he would not have escaped."

"How do you know?"

Martin said that so insincerely that Lena had a flash of knowledge. She was sure that he had something to do with Jam'elo's disappearance, but it wasn't until now that she fully understood what he'd done. He must have figured out some time ago that Jam'elo wasn't really a slave. Between that, and the knowledge that Lena would never be interested in him was what made him betray them. He must have sold Jam'elo— he would be prized—he was strong and in very good health.

"Martin, I know that you know that he wasn't a slave, so he would have nothing to 'escape' from. You had him kidnapped. You sold him, didn't you?"

"Why would I do such a thing?" Martin was a bad liar.

"Tell me who bought him from you!"

Martin remained silent, and then kicked his horse to gallop ahead of the wagon, which Emma was now driving. She knew one thing for sure. She wasn't going to pay him the last installment. He must have known that, because he disappeared over the next hill. Lena figured she'd not see him again. Lena knew how she would find Jam'elo.

Her first task was to get to the plantation, which was only a few miles distant. She'd drop off Clara and Robert Jr. at the plantation, then take her horse into town tomorrow, and find whoever was doing slave auctions, and find Jam'elo.

"Emma, let's go home. I'll find Jam'elo tomorrow."

"I din' trust that man, Mrs. Lena."

"I know, Emma. I shouldn't have ever trusted him either."

Richmond, VA, July 2, 1863/92 Musb 743

He had fallen asleep during the ride to Richmond. He was awakened by a kick to his head, and a shout, "Wake up!"

He was roughly taken off the horse, and at first, he had a hard time staying upright. He looked around him. He thought he must be inside the town of Richmond. They were in an alley behind a large building. One of the men grabbed the center of the shackles around his wrists, and dragged him into the building, which was very dimly lit. He couldn't see much at first, but he could tell there were a number of people there. He was taken through that room, into a front area, which had more light.

He thought that this front area must be where the auctions happened. There were seats, and a desk, and a sort of stage area. He was dragged toward one corner of the room, where a man sat at a desk strewn with paper.

"Who is this?" The man took a piece of paper and started writing.

The one who dragged him from the back said, "What's your name, boy?"

"Jam'elo Kadarin."

The man behind the desk asked, "What the hell kind of name is that?"

"It's my name."

"Where were you born?"

"I wasn't born in this country."

"You don't look old enough to have been born in Africa—besides, you are too light."

"I'm not Negro. I'm a foreigner."

The man next to him kicked him. "The hell you are."

The man behind the desk shook his head. "Why is it that you bring me all the weird ones? Now we have a first-class liar. I'm putting him down as Mulatto, birthplace unknown. Alright, strip him so I can see what scars and other problems he has."

The man next to him carefully undid one wrist shackle at a time as he took his shirt off, and one leg shackle at a time for the pants. The man who had been behind the desk came around to examine Jam'elo, up and down. He opened his mouth to look at his teeth.

"Since you say you are a foreigner, how long have you been in this country?"

"Three years."

The man shook his head. "Douglas, this man is too healthy to have been a slave. His teeth are *perfect*. Better than the mayor's. He has no scars. His hair is curly, not kinky. I'm not so sure he's lying, and if we sell him, and someone finds out he's not..."

"Shut up, no one will find out. We paid a pretty penny for him, and we can't afford to lose that. Someone will pay for him. He is a prized specimen. Besides, he ain't injun, chinee, or mexican. Gotta be a mulatto."

"Alright. I'll write it up. I don't think we should highlight him in the advertising tomorrow."

"Why not? Healthy, strong, Mulatto. That will work. I want to get a high price for him."

After they had examined Jam'elo, put his clothes back on him, and had an argument over how much to start his auction at, they dragged him to the back room, and put him in a corner. He understood that the auction was to happen in three days. They fastened his leg chains to another chain. He could walk in a relatively limited space, and it would be a chore, since the chains were heavy.

"If you need to relieve yourself, there is a hole over there," the man pointed to one corner of the room. He then walked out of the back door.

Jam'elo looked around him. There were six other people in the room, all of them in chains. Next to him was a woman and what looked to be her young son. She was staring at him.

"Hello," Jam'elo said to her. She was silent.

"She don't talk to no one." Jam'elo turned to face the man who spoke, sitting across from him.

"She never did talk. She and me, we from the same plantation."

"Why are you here?"

"Our Master went away and died in de war, and his wife done died of consumption. Their chillin don' want us—they move West."

Jam'elo though to himself about agent 21. So many people died of it.

"Why didn't they free you?"

The man laughed. "And lose de money? You a fool. What's your name?"

"Jam'elo. What's yours?"

"I'm Peter. You aren't a Mulatto, are you?"

"No, I'm not. I'm a foreigner."

"Those stupid people."

Jam'elo's stomach started to grumble. He hadn't eaten since the night before. He had no idea when he would eat next. He was also very thirsty.

"Is there any water?"

"They bring water around to drink twice a day with the food. That should be in a few hours."

The next few hours went very slowly. He talked with Peter for a while. Peter had been born and raised in Virginia, on the same plantation for many years. He'd gotten married and had several children. But then that plantation owner had died, and his family was split up, and he went to the second plantation, where he had just been. Peter had learned to read and had become an informal pastor to the slaves in his plantation, and several others around.

In fact, he knew the Miller plantation, and many of the slaves on it.

"I heard tell of that Lena Miller. It didn't surprise me that she fled. You say she come back?"

"Yes. Her brother died in the war, and her father died, so she's come back to take care of the plantation."

"And you know her how?"

"We traveled together from California."

"How did you end up here?"

"I was kidnapped."

Peter shook his head. "Stupid people. She care about you?"

Jam'elo was careful. "I expect so."

"Enough to buy you back?"

That thought had not occurred to Jam'elo—that Lena would find him and buy him back. That gave him hope that he would get to see her again.

"Yes, she might well." Jam'elo smiled.

Richmond, VA, July 3, 1863

She had ridden into town this morning and had left her horse at a stable in the outskirts of town. She was walking the few blocks to the slave auction house, where she expected to find Jam'elo. She hoped his night hadn't been too traumatic.

She was taking in the changes in Richmond since she left. There had been some growth, now that it served as a very important Confederate city. But it clearly had seen better days. She was passing a large open door —the door to a foundry, when she heard a snippet of a conversation that made her stop in her tracks.

"This looks like jewelry or something, but it's very strange. That metal is too strong to be steel, or even silver. But it's very bright and shiny. And this weird glass thing—I can't separate it from the metal."

"I think we should just toss it in the smelter. It will melt everything. Then, we can separate the different parts as they melt at different temperatures."

"That makes the most sense to me. Give it here."

Lena realized that they must be talking about Jam'elo's emergency communicator. She imagined they had obtained it from his kidnappers. She had no idea what would happen when it was melted. She imagined that it was strong, but she didn't know what it could withstand. She thought for a minute or two, then made a decision, and started to walk inside of the shop, when there was this enormous noise, she felt herself flying, and then knew nothing more.

She woke up in her bed, with a man looking over her.

"Ah, you are awake. That's very good."

"What happened?"

"You were caught in the explosion that destroyed the foundry and several buildings surrounding it. You were very lucky. About 10 people were killed."

"What time..."

"You've been unconscious for several hours."

She felt enormous pain and realized quickly that she was severely injured.

"You have been very badly injured. You must rest." The way he said it suggested that he wasn't quite sure she would survive.

"But I must, I must..."

"You must what, Mrs. Jameson?"

Lena started to cry. She needed Jam'elo.

"Is Mother here?"

"Yes, Lena, I'm here. You'll be alright. We'll take care of you."

"Can you please get someone to get Uncle George here. It's very important."

She trusted her uncle. He would do anything she asked him to.

"Lena, why? What's wrong?"

"Please, Mother, please."

"Alright dear, I'll get him. He's already on the plantation today—he wanted to see you."

In a few minutes, her uncle George was standing next to her bed.

"Ah, Lena, I'm so sorry to see you in this state. But you'll get better, I know."

Lena knew everyone was lying to her. She realized she was dying. She knew then that only Jam'elo could save her.

"Uncle, I need a big favor."

"You know I'll do whatever you want, dear."

"I need you to go to the auction house right now and buy me a man."

He frowned. "But there are plenty..."

"No, a *particular* man. It's a long story, but it's critical you buy him as soon as possible, and at whatever price they ask. I'll pay you back."

"My dear..."

"Really, Uncle, please? It's important, and I'll tell you the whole story later."

"Alright, I will do as you ask. Describe him."

"His name is Jam'elo Kadarin. He has light skin and curly hair. He is tall and has good teeth. He will probably be described by his sellers as mulatto or quadroon."

Her uncle looked puzzled, but she knew he would do as she asked.

"Alright. I'll leave right away. I'll let you know when I've bought him."

"Just bring him to me, please?"

"Alright, Lena."

"Mother, please have someone bring all of my things to this room—especially the largest chest."

"Lena, what do you need..."

"Please, Mother!"

"Alright, Lena, I will have that done immediately. I don't understand what's going on here."

"It will be alright, mother, I will survive."

She felt a wave of relief, and then she lost consciousness.

Richmond, VA, July 3, 1863/92 Musb 743

It had been a long night. Jam'elo drank the water that was offered, but the food smelled rotten, so he didn't eat it, since he didn't have any of his antibacterials with him. There were no blankets or any kind of padding on the floor, and the chains made getting comfortable impossible. Peter had become good company, and he had also talked with Lenore, Henry, and Katie. The woman and her child next to him remained silent.

He heard a huge explosion and screaming and yelling outside. It didn't seem especially close, but he had a feeling it was a large explosion. After a while, the man who had been behind the desk yesterday came into the room and looked around.

Peter said, "Sir, what was that?"

"The foundry exploded, a few blocks away. I saw it. It was the strangest kind of explosion. I've seen plenty in my life, but this was different. And no one can figure out how it happened—there weren't any weapons or gunpowder in the place."

Jam'elo asked, "What was strange about it?"

"The color. It wasn't orange and red with smoke. It was green and blue. There was smoke later, as the building began to burn, but not at first."

Jam'elo instantly knew what it had been. They had tried to melt his communicator. He guessed it was a quite logical thing for them to have done, but he couldn't help but shake his head.

He looked up to see Peter looking at him. When the man left, Peter said, "You know what happened, don'tcha?"

Jam'elo could only nod. "They stole something from me and tried to melt it."

Peter tilted his head. "You a strange man."

Jam'elo laughed and nodded. "Yes, Peter, I am."

The day continued much like the night before. Jam'elo was uncomfortable, dirty, and hungry. He wanted to see Lena. The longer the day wore on, the less hope he had that she would find him.

There wasn't much light in the room, but there was enough to gauge the time of day, and as evening approached, Jam'elo lost hope.

There was some reason Lena couldn't find him or wouldn't. He drifted to sleep.

He was awoken by the door to their room opening, and his name being called.

"Jam'elo, someone wants to buy you before the auction."

His heart sang. Lena!

The man came and unhooked the chain. "Come with me and meet him. Be nice. He wants to pay a good price. If you do anything that makes him not want you, you will be sorry, boy."

Jam'elo followed the man into the front room, which was now lit with lamps, as it was dark out. A short, squat man with a beard was standing in the room. Jam'elo looked around but didn't see Lena.

"Here he is."

"This is Jameelo Kadarin?"

"That's what he said his name was."

"Jameelo?"

"Yes, sir, that is me."

My niece asked me to buy you, but I'm confused. You certainly don't look like a mulatto."

"I am not. I am a foreigner."

"How did you end up being here?"

Jam'elo decided to be honest, but careful. "I traveled here with my employer, Mrs. Lena Jameson. The man who she had hired to guide us to Virginia from Texas betrayed us, and kidnapped me, and sold me to these people."

Jam'elo could sense the tension in the room grow. He imagined that this man was upset somehow at what had happened, and his captor was upset that what Jam'elo had said might be a problem for them.

This man, who he assumed was Lena's uncle, turned to the other man and said, "If this is true, you are doing an illegal sale. Because my niece wants this man freed, I will pay your price. But know this: the Richmond sheriff is a personal friend of mine, as is the mayor. I will make sure that you are investigated. Take off those shackles."

"But he might…"

"He has no reason to escape, since he never was a slave! Unchain him!"

The man unlocked the chains on his wrists and ankles. Jam'elo realized how uncomfortable he had been when he felt the relief of the shackles coming off. He looked at his wrists, and there were red, angry welts that went all around them.

"Come with me, Jameelo."

They left and got into a carriage. Jam'elo sat on the seat facing the man.

"I want to thank you for coming to get me, sir. What is your name?"

"I am George Miller, and as you probably have guessed, Lena is my niece. Unlike most people in this backwater, I've traveled around the world, in the military, and diplomatic corps. I've never seen quite the like of you, but I know you aren't a mulatto. And besides, your accent is strange. Where are you from?"

"It is called Casiti. You've never heard of it. Very small, and very far away."

George smiled. "It doesn't really matter. I also happen to know that Lena is not your employer, is she?"

Jam'elo chuckled quietly. "No, sir, she is not."

"Did she marry you?"

"No sir. I couldn't marry her. I have to go back home, and anyway, my people don't marry."

George shook his head, and they rode the rest of the way to the plantation in silence.

When they got to the plantation, and a man who Jam'elo assumed was a slave opened the door to the carriage, George said, "Follow me. Lena wants to see you right away. Just so you know, she has been badly injured in an explosion."

"The one at the foundry? What was she doing there?"

"I suspect she happened to be passing by. Had she been inside, she would be dead. As it is, the doctor says she will not survive."

Jam'elo knew he could save her. He wondered where his medical kit was. He'd deal with that after he saw Lena. He followed George up the stairs to a bedroom toward the back. George opened the door, and Jam'elo saw an older woman he assumed was Lena's mother, and an older man, who was examining Lena. He must be the doctor. He saw Lena unconscious in her bed.

Jam'elo asked, "When was she last awake? What is her condition?"

The doctor replied, "And who are you?"

George stepped in. "This is Jameelo Kadarin. He is the man Lena wanted released. He was kidnapped, and improperly sold. He is a foreigner."

"All well and good, but what business is Lena's condition to you?"

Jam'elo turned to George. "Sir, I need you to trust me. I know Lena must trust you, if she sent you to get me. I have skills that this doctor doesn't have, and I can treat her. She will survive and be fine. But I need you to trust me. I know that might be hard."

"No, it's not really. I've always known that Lena is a very good judge of character."

"Do you know where Lena's things are? My medical kit is among them."

"I certainly don't. Margaret?"

"Before she last went unconscious, she had me get a man to bring them all up. They are in that corner."

Jam'elo was relieved. Lena had enough presence of mind to make sure he had what he needed. She wasn't in imminent danger.

He went over to the corner, and found the chest that held his medical kit, as well as his other supplies. He realized he needed to clear the room.

"Sir, can you please escort the doctor and the lady out of this room? I need quiet to work."

Margaret said, "I'll be quiet, and I'll not leave my daughter's side. Certainly not leave her in the presence of this stranger!"

George said, "Margaret, this man is a stranger to us, but no stranger to Lena. Please, come with me. I trust him." He herded them out of the room. The doctor looked as if he would protest, but then decided otherwise. The door closed.

Jam'elo set to work. He realized that he needed to make sure she stayed asleep for a while, so he gave her an anesthetic. He would give her the antidote later.

He used his imager first, to assess the damage. She had type four burns over a lot of her body. Those he could treat easily, and he would do that last. Her skin would be very sensitive and itchy for a few days, but there was no way to avoid that. He kept going, as he knew she probably had internal injuries. He found fractures in her skull, femur, humerus, and pelvic bone. He saw that the fracture in her skull had severed some arteries in her meninges, and blood was beginning to accumulate. He needed to deal with that first. He took out a small device he hadn't used in a long while and programmed a set of nanomachines to deal with the bleeding in the meninges. He then looked at her internal organs and saw that she was bleeding internally in three other places. He programmed another set to deal with that.

He injected those nanomachines, and then went to work on the bone breaks. In his time here, he always set and splinted bone breaks, because it would seem far too miraculous for someone to heal almost immediately from a broken bone. The one exception had been when his horse broke a leg. But now, he didn't care, and he didn't think Lena would. He programmed a third set of nanomachines to deal with the bone breaks, and then injected them directly into the bone, very near the sites of the break.

He prepared the burn bandages and placed them over the burns. He then put a clean sheet over her, and a light blanket, put his medical equipment away, and then moved a chair right next to the bed. He should keep her asleep for about an hour. He could then wake her up.

He realized that if she had been injured so that she didn't wake up to ask for him, she would have died. With the techniques available to them, the doctors here could have done nothing. The doctor must have known, which is why he didn't object. He sat and looked at her beautiful face. He would be so sorry to leave, with so little time to say goodbye to her. He had an idea.

He took out his communicator and entered in the code for a synchronous connection. In a few minutes, a three-dimensional image of Her'ellen, his head teacher, popped up above his communicator.

"Jam'elo! We were worried about you. We missed your log entry and were preparing for contingencies. When your communicator stopped sending any locator signals, we sent two down to the surface to Richmond to look for you."

"I am fine, and safe. But my trip must end soon."

"Yes, indeed. We almost recalled you when you crossed the Mississippi river, but since your logs specifically asked us for tolerance, we relented. But you cannot stay there long, nor travel from there. We have data suggesting that there is fighting coming your way."

"I know. Can you give me two Reit'al weeks? I'd like to learn a little about life here, then I'll be ready to go."

"I think so. We will recall our people, and pick you up at 3rd hour, 103 Musb. However, if danger comes close, we may retrieve you sooner."

"Understood."

He now had a little time to spend with Lena and say a longer goodbye. He took out his imager again and looked her over. She was healing rapidly. The internal bleeding had stopped, and most of the excess blood had been eliminated, her bones were knitting, and her burns were healing rapidly. She would be able to walk in a couple of hours. He smiled as he put two drops of anesthetic antidote in her mouth.

Her eyelids fluttered, and Jam'elo put his hand on her forehead, and stroked her hair.

"Hey love, I'm here."

"Jam'elo..."

"Relax. It will be a couple of hours before you should get up. Rest will be good for you. You might as well sleep the night before you get up."

She laughed lightly. "Two hours?"

"Yes."

"I was going to die, wasn't I?"

"Yes."

"You didn't temper the treatment, did you?"

"No. Should I have?"

She laughed again. "Of course not. I know that I have only a couple of days left with you."

"Actually, we have two weeks. I asked my teacher for an extension, and he gave it."

"Come to bed with me."

"Is that a good idea, Lena? Your mother..."

"I want you in my bed every night of those two weeks, my mother be damned."

Jam'elo chuckled. "Well, before then, I need to get your mother, uncle and doctor in here so they can talk with you and be sure I didn't kill you. You can explain it to your mother."

Jam'elo got up, and opened the door, to see the three of them sitting in chairs outside. He should have realized that they would be waiting right outside the door. They probably heard his exchange with Her'ellen, although they would not have been able to understand it.

"Lena would like to see you."

Lena's mother and the doctor rushed into the room, and George stayed behind.

"Jameelo, I could swear I heard a different voice, and we definitely heard you speak in another language."

"Military secret, sir. But don't worry, I'm not Union. Totally different situation." Jam'elo had gotten pretty good at pretending.

George didn't quite look satisfied, but he didn't press the point. They both returned to the room to see the doctor looking over the burn bandages and asking Lena how she felt.

When she saw Jam'elo re-enter the room, she asked him, "Jam'elo, my skin under these bandages itches terribly. Is that right?"

"Ah, it means it's time to take them off. Excuse me, please."

He carefully removed the bandages from her skin, while the doctor looked on. He removed them from her arms and torso, to reveal new, pink skin. The doctor gasped.

"Lena, this skin will be itchy and sensitive for a few days. There's not much I can do about that. But you'll be back to normal within a week."

The doctor turned to look at Jam'elo with a look on his face that was unreadable. He asked, "How did you do that?"

Lena answered before Jam'elo could. "He can do magic, doctor."

The doctor then looked at Jam'elo with a combination of awe and fear. Jam'elo guessed the fear won out, because the doctor went running from the room. Lena clearly enjoyed herself.

"Mother, please have someone show Jam'elo to a bath, and get him something to eat. I imagine he hasn't eaten well in his captivity. I know that you might think differently, but Jam'elo is to be respected. He is a foreigner. He will be staying here with me."

Jam'elo heard a sharp intake of breath.

Margaret said loudly and with some indignation, "Lena, how dare you..."

"Mother, you asked me here to help you run things. I reluctantly left my quiet life with Jam'elo in California to come all the way back here and help you. He has to leave to go back to his home in two weeks. If you aren't willing to do as I ask, we will be leaving in the morning."

"Lena..."

"Mother."

"As you wish." She left the room and returned quickly with one of the house servants.

"Jordan, please show Mr. Jameelo here a place to bathe, and give him dinner."

"Yes ma'am. Sir, if you will follow me..."

Richmond, VA, July 4, 1863/93 Musb 743

Jam'elo woke to Lena stroking his face. He opened his eyes, and wondered if it all had been a long, scary dream. Were they still in San Francisco? He looked around the room and knew it had been no dream.

Jam'elo looked at Lena. "How are you feeling, dear heart?"

"I am fine, thanks to you. It's quite late—I've already been up and about. When mother saw me walking around, she looked like she had seen a ghost." Lena smiled.

"Well, from her perspective, you might as well be. I'm so glad I could save you. I shudder to think that I might have gotten rescued, and never known that you had died!" He could feel the tears welling in his eyes.

"Did you think anything short of dying would have stopped me from getting to you somehow?"

He smiled, and she kissed the tears from his cheeks.

She said, "We have two weeks to say a proper goodbye. Thank you for requesting that."

"How could I not? I had to make sure that you got well, after all." He smiled.

She said, "I wonder how Emma is doing with all this?"

Jam'elo answered, "Lena, I did a lot of thinking about her while I was in that auction house. I spent a lot of time talking with the others there. When I thought that I wouldn't get to see you again, I thought about what her life would be like. I knew that you would take as good care of her as you could, but you would only have so much control. She doesn't really belong anywhere."

Lena nodded. "Her life here in Virginia will be difficult for her, and she won't really be able to go anywhere else. And now that she's met you, and knows some of what you know, nothing will ever satisfy her. I think you should take her back with you."

He said, "You think so?"

Lena nodded vigorously.

"I think you are right my love. Ah, one more thing to negotiate with my teachers."

"She will flower on Casiti, Jam'elo."

He nodded. He knew this was so. They were silent for a while.

Lena said, "Make love to me Jam'elo. We haven't shared a bed in so long..."

"You probably should..." she shut him up by kissing him fiercely, and all of his resistance on her behalf melted away as he felt the strength of her desire. All of the weeks of travel, of distance, of stress, of pretending to be something else to each other, melted away as they moved together in the rhythm of their love.

Richmond VA, July 4, 1863

Emma woke and was again surprised by the comfort of the bed she was sleeping on. She luxuriated in the feeling of the bed for a few more minutes, and then decided to get up and find something to eat.

Arriving at Lena's home plantation had been somewhat surrealistic to Emma. Emma was free, and Lena had insisted that Emma be treated as a guest, and given a guest room, instead of being boarded with the other slaves.

What surprised Emma was that the slaves that she had encountered were not in any way resentful of her. In fact, there had been a kind of quiet jubilance in the air when Lena arrived. It had been tempered greatly when she was so badly injured, but once Jam'elo returned, and it was clear late last night that Lena would be fine, the jubilance had returned. And because Emma had some part in Lena's return, she was treated with great kindness.

Emma had talked at length with Lena, and she knew that Lena would free the slaves almost immediately on her return. Emma had not told anyone of that knowledge, but it seemed that somehow, they all knew this would happen. Those that had been here while Lena was growing up knew what kind of woman she was.

Emma used the water in the basin to do a quick clean up, and then got dressed. She walked downstairs, toward where she remembered the kitchen was. She was intercepted by the man who had told her his name was Jordan.

"Good morning, Miss Emma. You don' need to go to the kitchen. There is breakfast in the sunroom for you, Jam'elo and Lena, when they get up."

Emma didn't quite know what to say, but she managed to stammer, "Thank... thank you, Mr. Jordan. I 'preciate it."

He nodded and pointed the way to the sunroom. She walked into the room that had large windows on three sides, a glass roof, and potted plants all around. There was a table in the center that was set for three, and a sideboard that was filled with what looked like delicious food—food that Emma had never, ever been able to eat in her life, save in little scraps or old leftovers.

There was sausage and eggs, and some beautiful looking pastries, and other delicacies that she knew had been imported from somewhere far away. She took a plate from the table and loaded it up with a lot of food. She was hungry, and although she had eaten a nice dinner last night, she felt famished.

She was just about to sit down to eat, when she heard Jam'elo's voice.

"Thank you, Jordan, and thank you for your help last night."

"It's nice to see missus Lena doing so well."

Emma heard Lena say, "It's so nice to see you, Jordan. I hope you have been well while I've been away."

"I been doing alright, but I'm glad you are back missus Lena."

"Thank you, Jordan."

Emma watched Jam'elo and Lena walk into the sunroom. She noticed that they seemed happy. That made her happy.

Jam'elo said, smiling, "Good morning, Emma."

"Good morning, Jameelo. It's nice ta see you looking good Missus Lena. A lot o' people were very worried 'bout you."

"Thank you, Emma, I'm glad to be doing so well. Jam'elo here is the reason. He saved my life, yet again."

Lena and Jam'elo both went to the sideboard, and gathered up food, and the three of them sat down at the table to eat.

Jam'elo looked around, and said, "This room reminds me so much of the greenhouses we have in all of our homes. Except that we don't have breakfast in them." He smiled.

Emma asked, "Why do you have greenhouses, Jameelo?"

"Since we have such long winters, we grow a lot of food during the winter in the greenhouses. Also, we use them to grow seedlings that we plant in spring. And in the high summer, we use the greenhouses to grow flowers."

Emma said, "Your home sounds so... so wonderful, Jameelo. I wish I could see it."

She realized as she said it, she really felt it. She wanted more than anything to leave here, go to the stars, and see his home planet. A sadness descended on her, and she looked down at her empty plate. Her life felt like that plate, empty of hope. Yes, she was free, but what did that mean? What hope did she have of doing the kinds of things she really wanted to do—learn astronomy and study the stars? The wonderful breakfast now sat like a lump in her stomach.

There was silence for a while, and she looked up to see Jam'elo looking at her.

In a while, he said quietly, "Is that what you really want?"

She looked at him with surprise, and then wondered whether he was playing with her. Then with relief she remembered that he was not that kind of man.

"Yes, Jameelo, I want dat. More than anythin' I ever wanted."

He smiled. "Then you shall have it. I'll bring you with me. Understand that you'll never be able to come back."

She felt a feeling coursing through her that was utterly unfamiliar. It made her fingers tingle, and she started to breathe fast. She realized that she was happy. She laughed.

"Come back? Why would I wanna evah come back, Jameelo?" Jam'elo and Lena laughed with her.

Lena said, "Emma, I'm glad you want to go."

"Missus Lena, don' you wanna go?"

Lena gave Emma a half smile. "Emma, I don't want to let Jam'elo go. I wish I could be with him every day of the rest of my life. But my life, my world, is here. Unlike you, I'm not meant to leave, or go to the stars. I'm meant to stay, raise my children, and do the best I can do here. I have my work cut out for me."

Emma nodded, and they started to talk about the plantation, and what Lena was going to do next. Emma did not envy her one bit. And the sheer joy that she was leaving and going to the stars stayed with her.

Richmond, VA, July 4, 1863/93 Musb 743

Jam'elo sat on the porch, watching the activities around the house as the afternoon wore into evening. It was, in its own way, a bucolic setting. The grounds were very well tended, the trees provided ample shade for the heat of the afternoon, and the birds were chirping happily, as if this were some kind of paradise.

Jam'elo had met three slaves so far, all house servants. He hadn't had a chance to talk with them yet, but he would try to find time to hear and record their stories before he left. Lena had promised him a tour of the plantation tomorrow—she felt she needed to look around at how things were, and she also wanted to meet all of the slaves who had arrived since she left nine years ago.

Jam'elo knew that she intended to free them all, probably before he left. He could only imagine how her mother would feel about that.

He heard the sound of the footsteps next to him. He looked over to see Mrs. Miller looking at him. She walked to the chair next to his on the porch and sat down.

"What do you think of our lovely plantation, Mr. Jameelo?" He didn't feel like it was right to correct her at this moment, especially since he felt that he was about to offend her with his answer.

"Mrs. Miller, I don't want to insult you, and I don't want to lie, so shall we just let that question go by the by?"

"I take it you feel as my daughter does."

"Yes. A very, very long time ago, long before this continent was settled by your ancestors, my people were enslaved. We have never forgotten the experience that forged us. I cannot find a way to condone what you are doing here."

"Well, in that you have plenty of company. I expect the Union will win this war, and all of the slaves will be freed in the South. Lena has said she plans to release our slaves immediately. At this point, I don't really care anymore. My only son is dead in this horrible war, and my husband is dead too. The only people I have in this world are Lena and George. And both of them hate slavery."

There was silence for a while. He heard in the distance the sound of children. It had been so long since he'd been able to spend time with Clara and Robert Jr. He'd missed them. He got up just as Lena and the children came onto the porch.

"Jameelo!" Clara ran to him and they hugged. "We missed you. Mother says we can stop pretending now."

Jam'elo looked up at Lena, and then smiled at Clara. "Yes, Clara. No more pretending. And I'll only be here for two more weeks, so I have to finish teaching you that math problem I promised to."

"Why are you leaving, Jam'elo? Don't you want to stay here with us?"

He could feel her sadness, and he felt tears on his cheek.

"Little one, I would love to stay with you, but I have to go home. This isn't my home. My home is far away, and my own family is waiting to see me."

"Can I come?"

Jam'elo couldn't help but smile. He had come to love Clara dearly, almost as if she were his own daughter. The same was true for Robert Jr. He felt, at some level that they were his children as well as Lena's.

He squatted down so that they were at eye level. "Clara, your home is here, and you need to stay. I know that you will do great things." And he did really know it.

Chapter 8

Expedition Log 743.5.15 Student: Jam'elo z Kadarin, 94 Musb 743

It is finally time for me to bring this expedition to a close. I am being picked up in 9 days and I will say my final goodbye to Lena Jameson, who I have become close to.

I have learned a lot about slavery since my last log. I was kidnapped and sold as a slave and spent some hours among a few slaves who were being sold at auction. I have also continued to learn from Emma.

I have sent in my official request to bring Emma with me to Casiti and have heard that it has been approved. We have talked a little bit about what it will be like, but she is being uncharacteristically quiet—she has asked few questions. I'm not sure exactly why that is, but I imagine that she is getting used to the idea that her life is going to be utterly different than what it has been.

I will be recording stories of the slaves here on Lena's plantation, and getting to learn more about how it works, and what people do here. I am almost ready to go home.

Attached are climate data for this last period.

Richmond, VA, July 5, 1863

Martin left the bar, a little tipsy. He hurried down toward the auction house, since he knew the auction was about to start. He was happy that he would get to see Jam'elo sold to someone. He opened the door, and walked in, and took a seat toward the back.

As he waited for things to settle down, he looked around at the buyers. He knew some of these—friends of his father. Well, former friends of his father—they no longer socialized with him, now that he had nothing.

"First in line is Peter. A strong man and very obedient. He knows blacksmithing and works well with tobacco or cotton farming. He also has some experience as a foreman."

The auction continued, first with this man Peter, then a woman and her child, then some others. It finally became clear, once the auction was about to end, that Jam'elo was nowhere in sight. He felt foolish. Of course, Lena knew where to find him, and she had enough money to buy him back.

He walked back to the bar and sat in the stool he had just left an hour or so ago.

"What'll it be, sir?"

"Just whiskey."

He sat and nursed his drink for a bit, then gulped it down, and ordered another. The money he had gotten for Jam'elo was ten times what Lena owed him for the guide work he did. Of course, he never expected to demand that, or get paid for it. But what he got wasn't enough to do much in Richmond. He wanted to stay, though, and make his way here. But he didn't know how. He didn't have enough money to buy a farm or plantation, or any slaves. He didn't even have enough money to make wooing any lady of a plantation a reality. He couldn't help but wonder what the whole point had been.

Richmond, VA, July 5, 1863

Lena and Jam'elo were riding their horses back toward the main house after the tour of the plantation. Lena was in a very foul mood, and Jam'elo had been quiet for most of the tour. Lena had met Walter, the new field foreman. He was a nasty man. The only reason Lena hadn't fired him on the spot was that she knew she would need his help to identify all of the slaves, so that the process of freeing them could go smoothly. She knew her mother would defend him, but some of what Lena had heard about what he'd done was indefensible. Walter had also gone out of his way to be disrespectful toward Jam'elo.

She had been surprised to find out how few slaves were left that she knew. There had been an outbreak of some sort four years ago, and many of the slaves had died. Between that and Walter's brutality, the attrition rate of the field hands had been horrific. Paul, one of the oldest slaves, was still around, and had told her that at least 10 slaves owed their death to Walter's lash.

She didn't let on that she was freeing them quite yet, although she got the impression that somehow, they already knew. She wanted to get everything prepared —the supplies and money she would provide for those who wanted to leave, and the employment details for those who wanted to stay. It wasn't a great time for free Negroes in the South right now and getting North would be difficult. But she knew that at least some of the younger men would want to go North to fight in the Union army, now that they were accepting Negro soldiers.

"You've been quiet, dear heart." Jam'elo's voice stirred her out of her thoughts.

"I have a lot to think about. I'm appalled at what's happened to the slaves here while I was gone, and I'm trying to plan how to free them all."

"What is there to figure out?"

Jam'elo often surprised her with his naïveté.

"Well, I need to make sure that I am able to give all of them something that will help them survive. And some of them will want to stay, so I have to figure out how I am going to manage to afford to pay them a decent wage."

Jam'elo smiled. "I see. You are being extraordinarily generous, which doesn't surprise me. The slave I met while I was captured told me a story of a plantation owner who freed his slaves right after the Emancipation Proclamation. He just let them go to fend for themselves. That seems more normal to me."

Lena chuckled, and remembered she often had to re-evaluate her perceptions about what Jam'elo understood about their culture.

Richmond, VA, July 17, 1863/103 Musb 743

Lena and Jam'elo sat together on the porch. They had spent most of the last night and this morning making love and talking, and never wanting it to end. Next to Jam'elo was his medical kit, a box of artifacts he was taking back with him, and a basket of food Lena had insisted on putting together for him. He said the trip to his ship in orbit would take about 15 minutes, but she could hardly believe that, and she wanted him to have good food with him for the journey.

Jam'elo had spent the last two hours with Clara and Robert Jr. saying goodbye. Both of them had been inconsolable, and Lena was sure that she would be comforting them for months. Lena had asked all of the house servants, who were now employees, to stay away from the front of the house until 2:00, which was after Jam'elo would have left. Jam'elo had said there wasn't going to be much to see, but he was grateful that she wanted to be careful.

"Jam'elo, I have something for you." Jam'elo looked at her, and she could see the tears in his eyes.

"What is it?"

She took out of her sleeve the pocket watch that she had been meaning to give to him for months. She'd gotten it engraved in San Francisco, but there hadn't seemed to be an appropriate time before now to give it to him.

"I had something engraved inside."

Jam'elo took the watch and opened the cover to look inside. He looked at her with such tenderness that she thought she would melt into a puddle on the porch.

"I will treasure this always."

"Will you do me a favor?"

"Anything, my love."

"When the time comes, as you've said it must, when your people let our people know that you are out there, can you make sure that this watch makes its way back to my family? I want them to know about us."

Jam'elo smiled. "Yes, my love. I will make that happen."

Lena heard footsteps and saw Emma walking onto the porch. She had outfitted her with a new man's suit, and one of the other slaves in the plantation had given her a haircut. Lena looked at Jam'elo, who was smiling.

Lena got up, took Emma by the shoulders, and held her at arm's length.

"Emma, you certainly look good in those clothes."

"Thank you, missus Lena. Dey sure feel good."

It was interesting to Lena that she had felt an instinctual need to give Emma new clothes, and the clothes that came to mind to her were men's clothes. It seemed almost uncharacteristic of herself, but she shook it off.

Lena heard a beep, and Jam'elo took out a device, and looked at it, and put it back in his pocket.

"Love, it's time for us to go."

Lena nodded, and she could feel the tears pooling in her eyes.

"You should stay on the porch."

Lena nodded again. She felt more than saw Jam'elo come close to her, and they embraced for one last time.

"I will always remember you, Lena. I will always love you."

She was sniffing and knew that soon she would be weeping.

"I will always love you, Jam'elo. Be well. I will look at Orion each night in the winter and know that you are well."

She heard a sound she could not identify, and Jam'elo broke the embrace. She wiped her eyes, and saw an oblong shape appear in the middle of the front yard.

"That's our ride home, Emma."

Lena stayed on the porch and watched them walk down toward the oblong shape. Emma entered the shape and disappeared. Jam'elo turned back, and blew her a kiss, and disappeared himself. The oblong shape closed up, and she felt a wind blow, and heard that sound again, and then it was all quiet. Jam'elo and Emma were gone forever.

She sat on the porch crying for a little bit. She finally got up and went inside to start the long process of taking care of things.

Richmond, VA, September 5, 1863

Martin was on his horse, riding toward the Miller plantation. In his saddlebag was a package for Lena Jameson. It was the money he had made from the sale of Jam'elo, minus the remainder of his guiding fee.

He had spent the last two months mostly drunk, and when he wasn't drunk, he was full of remorse for what he had done. He knew that he could never really make up for the hurt he had caused but giving the money back to Lena was the best he could think of.

In his sober moments, he remembered how well Jam'elo had treated him, even though Martin treated him badly. He remembered Jam'elo saving Edwin's life and saving his own when they had almost lost everything in that washout in western Mississippi.

He had assumed that his return to Virginia would be triumphant—it was anything but. His father was still a pariah, and thus he was. Richmond was economically falling apart, and there were no opportunities for him to make anything of his new money. He realized, finally, that Virginia wasn't home anymore, and he should return to the West, where he could make his life anew. He was heading to St. Louis, where he hoped he could attach himself to a wagon train going west. He remembered what Lena had said about Oregon and thought that might be a good destination.

He rode up the long road to the Miller plantation and was looking for the first person he could find to hand this package off to, so he could leave as quickly as he could without seeing Lena.

He saw a slave in front of the large plantation house sweeping the steps. He looked like a good candidate.

"Hey, you! I have a package for your mistress." The man turned toward him and frowned.

"You mean Mrs. Lena? She ain't my mistress. She's my employer. You have something for her?"

Martin was taken aback by this man's attitude toward him, and what he said. It didn't matter. He needed to get rid of this package.

He took the package from his saddlebag and bent down on his horse to give it to the man.

"See that Mrs. Lena Jameson gets this package."

"What is it that you could possibly give me, Martin?" Martin looked up to see Lena on the porch, looking at him. This is just what he had wanted to avoid.

"It's the money I owe you—all the money I got for selling Jam'elo, minus what was left of my guiding fee. I'm... I'm... I'm sorry I betrayed you. It wasn't my better nature."

"Martin, where are you headed?" He was surprised by that question. He had expected invective. Lena looked at him with what he thought was pity. He didn't want her pity.

150

"I'm leaving, Mrs. Jameson. Virginia isn't the place for me, it turns out. I'm going back West. Might even move to Oregon."

She nodded. "Jordan, please give Martin his package back. Martin, I don't need that money, and the deed is done. I imagine you need it more than I do. In the end, no harm was done by your action, but of course you had no way of knowing that. Jam'elo is gone. He went home."

"But Mrs. Jameson, I need to give you this money—I need to make up for what I have done."

"Martin, you can make up for what you have done by treating everyone, including coloreds, with respect. Can you do that?"

He didn't know what to say, except to nod.

He then managed, "I'll do my best."

"That's all I ask. Good luck, Martin."

Kor'lova, Rel'toro, Casiti, 50 Nird 744

Emma sat next to Jam'elo in the small vehicle that was taking them to the house of Jam'elo's friend. There were some things that still scared Emma, including riding in these things at speeds that were hard for her to imagine. Not even trains went this fast, and she'd only seen one train in her life.

She had been on Casiti for a couple of months Earth time. For a while, it had just seemed like a very long dream, but every time she woke up in her new bed, she realized that it was true—she was not on Earth anymore.

She went outside every night to look at the stars, although at this time of year the sky was often cloudy. When she could see the stars, it also reminded her how far away she was from home —none of the constellations were the same.

One of the most surprising things was how everyone looked just like Jam'elo. Not really like Jam'elo, but they all had the same kind of hair and eyes and skin color. Some were a slightly lighter color, and some were slightly darker. She obviously stood out among them, with her dark skin color and kinky hair, which felt strange to her. And, of course, everyone she met knew her story. They were all very respectful of her privacy, but she felt the curiosity from them.

"We are almost there, Emma."

She nodded. Jam'elo had told her a lot about her friend, and one time companion, Re'ten. They were going to spend a few days with him, and he was going to interview her. She was looking forward to telling someone the whole story, finally. She felt that once this was over, she could start moving on, and figuring out what she was going to do with the rest of her life, which was going to be a lot longer than she could have ever imagined. Jam'elo told her that the average life expectancy on Casiti was 150 Earth years.

"Jam'elo, I wanna go ta school. Dere a school I can go?"

"Emma, education here is different than it is on Earth. We don't really have schools. Children learn from adults in their family groups as they grow up. While they are in the youth communities, they explore the kinds of work they might want to do by being apprentices in as many fields as they want, each for one Casitian month. Then they choose and become a student under a particular teacher."

"Jam'elo, I know what I wanna do."

Jam'elo smiled at her. "Emma, astronomy is not the same kind of science it is on Earth. On Earth, astronomy is mostly math and physics. Here, there is math and physics, but a host of other things. You can do galactic mapping, join exploratory teams, study planetary geology, or study galactic biology."

Emma let that sink in for a little bit. She realized she had no idea what she wanted to do, short of working to answer the whole host of questions she had about things. She realized that the Casitians probably had a lot of the answers already.

"Alright, Jam'elo. I guess I gotta start from the beginning, huh?"

Jam'elo said, "Yes, Emma, you do. And I have just the teacher for you."

"Who dat?"

"My brother, Lam'il. I've already told him about you, and he is excited to meet you, and teach you. He is one of us who has never been happy settling down into one field—he has done several in his life, and I expect that he will do more. But right now, his work is helping those in youth communities figure out their paths. He has some innovative ideas on how to make it easier for them."

"Thank you Jam'elo. I would be happy to study with Lam'il."

The vehicle slowed, and went through a few small alleyways between dwellings, and came to a stop in front of a dwelling that was connected to others in a semi-circle. This had a small center area, where she saw children playing in the snow—even though it was colder outside than Emma had ever experienced. They got out of the vehicle, and Emma saw Jam'elo push a button that resulted in a quiet chime inside the house. The door opened and a man answered it. Emma thought that must be Jam'elo's friend, Re'ten.

The man said something that Emma couldn't yet understand.

They walked into the dwelling, and Emma saw a woman get up to greet them, who Jam'elo said was Yar'li, Re'ten's current companion. Jam'elo and Re'ten shared a long hug, and then he went to hug Yar'li.

Jam'elo said something in Casitian, then translated, "Re'ten, Yar'li, please meet Emma."

Emma stuck her hand out to shake with Re'ten, but he didn't shake her hand. Jam'elo said something in Casitian, and Re'ten put out his hand, and Emma clasped it, they shook hands somewhat awkwardly. Yar'li shook hands with Emma as well.

Emma said, in English, "Nice to meet you."

Richmond, VA, July 17, 1873

Lena walked into Clara's room with the package that had just been delivered from the tailor's shop.

"Clara, here are the shirts I ordered for you. That should be the last of it."

"Yes, Mother, and I'm almost finished packing."

"Well, that's a good thing, since the train is leaving tomorrow morning! I have to admit I was worried about whether you would manage to get ready in time."

"Mother!" Clara looked indignant, and then they both broke out laughing.

"Mother, I'll miss you in Massachusetts."

"I know Clara. And I will miss you terribly. But I couldn't stand the idea of you staying here. This isn't the place for you."

"I know. I'm looking forward to being in school."

"Mount Holyoke Seminary will be good for you, Clara."

They talked for a while about what her life might be like, and what she might try to do. Lena knew that Clara wanted to be a teacher, and Lena would do all that she could to help Clara with that dream.

Lena for a moment reflected on her two children, and what they had become. Clara was strong-willed—even more strong-willed than Lena herself. She talked about injustice wherever she saw it, whether it was the treatment of negroes, that women couldn't vote, or the war orphans who weren't getting food or a place to stay.

Robert Jr., on the other hand, had a quiet heart and a quiet mind. He had taken to the techniques Jam'elo had taught him, and still practiced them avidly to this day. She imagined he would practice them his whole life. He saw injustice just like Clara, but he didn't say much about it, but treated everyone with a respect that Lena thought remarkable.

He had thrown himself into learning the ropes of the plantation, even though he was only fifteen. He worked alongside the field hands, who were now employees, and had become a very able farmer. He had already made it clear to her that he wanted to stay and work on the plantation, and she was happy to have him stay.

Clara pulled her out of her thoughts by saying, "I wonder how Emma is, Mother. I'm sure Jam'elo is fine, because he is home, but I wonder how Emma is getting along."

Lena nodded. "Yes, Clara, I wonder that too."

Hol'venif, Rel'toro, Casiti, 134 Musb 746

Em'ela woke, and looked over at Ja'leri, who was still sleeping soundly, her breaths moving the hairs that had fallen in front of her face. Em'ela envied Ja'leri her ability to sleep later than sunrise. For Em'ela the rise of the sun still seemed to be a cue to her body to arise, even though there was no real need.

She quietly rose from the bed and went into the kitchen to make herself a cup of fuge. Mornings were the hardest time for Em'ela, the time when her sadness was most likely to visit. She could remember mornings at the Kildare plantation, where she would be getting her daughter up and getting her breakfast before she started her workday in the house. It had been a long time since she had seen her daughter last. It had been, by her calculation, just over fifteen years. Her daughter would be twenty-three. And adult, and possibly married with children.

Before she and Jam'elo left, Lena had told her that she was sure that the war would be won by the North, and that the slaves would eventually be freed. That gave her hope that perhaps May would have the chance at a decent life.

The sadness faded, and the excitement of her new project took over her mind. She had, after several apprenticeships, finally settled on stellar dynamics as her field of study. She loved the work, and she was presently analyzing the data from the probe sent to a star that was approximately one year from becoming a nova. She looked forward to writing the paper about it—she had a novel theory, one that she was eager to prove. She thought this last crop of data would help.

Sometimes, even though she had been on Casiti for 12 Earth years, it was hard for her to reconcile her two lives. She had lived a life of hardship hardly imaginable by her friends on Casiti, and she now lived a life of luxury and freedom she could never have imagined when she was on Earth. She had taken a new name, Em'ela z Kadarin, was now fluent in spoken and written Casitian, and she had learned a lot of astronomy and science. She had even taken a female companion, something she could not have ever imagined happening at home. Everything was different.

In about 17 Casitian years, the next expedition would go to Earth, in the year 1940. She would be 103, too old to go, and in any event, she knew that they would never allow it. But she would find out about what kind of place her country had become in that time. Would slavery truly be over? Would her people be finally equal? Would her daughter's daughter be able to study stellar dynamics? She looked forward to finding out. And perhaps she would find out what happened to her daughter.

Epilogue

Francis was annoyed this morning. She had to finally finish cleaning out her mother's storage locker in Concord. Her mother had died one and a half years ago, just at the height of the Casitian Crisis, and Francis had delayed dealing with her mother's effects until things settled down. The whole fiasco with her ex-husband who went with their church to New Earth had been deeply unsettling. They had been close to divorcing before, so she had been very surprised at his degree of anger when she refused to accompany him to that silly colony.

As she drove the two hours in the rental truck from her home in Northampton to Concord, she thought about what had occurred over the past few years. She had a new life, now. She was single, and one of her children stayed on Earth, while the other went with his father to New Earth. She imagined she'd never see either of them again.

Her son William seemed to have responded to her liberalness with a conservativeness that exceeded her husband's. It never quite made any sense to her. She had always seen in him leadership qualities and tried to nurture them. It was sad to think that she wouldn't ever see what kind of leader William would become, but on the other hand, perhaps she would not have wanted to know.

She arrived at the storage facility and went to her mother's locker. She'd been there years ago, before her mother died. Francis knew it was filled with stuff, most of it garbage. She had hired a couple of guys to help her sort out what was garbage, and what she would take with her back to Northampton. They were going to meet her here in an hour. In the meantime, she could at least start the process.

Several hours later, there wasn't much left in the locker. In the far corner sat a very old chest. She had never seen it before. She didn't want to open it now—it looked like it certainly should come home with her.

The next day, she was sitting in her living room, with a few of the most interesting items scattered about.

"Whose chest do you think that was, Mom?"

Her son Peter had helped her unload the truck and was sitting with her in the living room.

"I have no idea. Perhaps we should open it up and find out, eh?"

It had a rusty lock on it, which was closed, but it was so corroded that Francis just pulled on it, and it fell apart. She wondered how long it had been locked. She opened up the top of the chest, and she could see that it was filled with all sorts of things that looked very old.

"This looks to be 19th century stuff. I wonder if it belonged to my mother's great-grandmother. She talked a lot about Clara Liebling, who lived to be a very old woman. I learned that she was a very famous activist and organizer. She played a pivotal role late in her life in getting women the vote. I was interviewed for her biography about ten years ago."

They spent some time looking though the chest, and they found a package of letters held together with string. As Francis opened them, she saw that they were all addressed to Clara Jameson, or Clara Jameson Liebling. The return address was always from Lena Jameson, Richmond, Virginia.

"Wow, this is really interesting—letters from Lena Jameson to Clara. Lena must be her mother. I'm sure there are some historians who would love to get hold of these letters."

Francis spent the next several days reading the letters. She was astounded at what she read. Some of the letters were mundane: Lena talking about life in Richmond during reconstruction, asking Clara about life in Massachusetts, Clara talking about her activism and politics. But a large portion of the content of the letters were stories about a man named Jam'elo, and a slave woman called Emma. The letters made it clear that both Clara and Lena knew Jam'elo was from another planet, and that he had taken the slave woman with him and left Earth. Finally, in one letter, it was spelled out—he was from Casiti! It was so strange, yet now in the light of what had happened over the past few years, it made so much sense. She needed to get in touch with someone at the Casitian liaison office.

Ja'el z Kadarin sat across from Francis, and Marianne Michaelson brought cups of a hot drink they called fuge and sat down with them at the table. It was strange to Francis to be in the same room with these two—they were legends on Earth.

Ja'el started the conversation. "Thank you so much for coming to Casiti to visit and letting us duplicate the letters. My great-great-great grandmother Selena was Jam'elo's mother. It answers some questions that our historians have had about what Jam'elo did on Earth, and it helps us in our family group understand more about our dear one. I hadn't been aware of this history in my family until I did some research after you got in contact with us. It's nice to hear Lena and Clara's side of Jam'elo's story. It had been clear from what we knew that he loved them dearly. It's clear that love was mutual."

Francis said, "I don't quite know what I would have made of the letters had I found them before you came to Earth, and before I knew about Casiti. It is a story that would have seemed so... so farfetched."

"Yes, I can imagine it would have. But Casitians had been visiting Earth every 20 Casitian years for hundreds of years before we made public contact a few years ago. I do expect that this particular expedition was one of the most... extraordinary."

Marianne said, "I'm struck by what kind of experience Jam'elo would have had on Earth at that time, looking like a Casitian, and experiencing slavery firsthand. I'm looking forward to digging into his logs and diaries, and the analyses of Casitian historians. And I'm especially interested in learning more about Emma. The little bit I've found suggests she became a well-regarded scientist."

She added, looking at Ja'el, "And it's interesting to know that we aren't the first Terran/Casitian companions."

Ja'el smiled. "Yes, there were precedents set before us. Which reminds me..." Ja'el got up to go to her desk and picked up a small box.

"One of the major reasons I had wanted you to come to Casiti is to present you with this. This object has been sitting in the Center for many years—it was given to them by my family when Jam'elo died. He had made a special request that it be given back to your family when we made full contact with Terrans."

Francis took the box, and opened it up, and pulled out a beautifully engraved pocket watch.

Francis said, "It's a pocket watch."

Ja'el asked, "A what?"

Marianne said, "Ja'el, before everyone used their cell phones for timekeeping, and before people wore timepieces on their wrists, this was a very common thing for men to carry to keep track of time."

Ja'el said, "Ah, it's a chronometer. Open it up. There is an interesting engraving."

Francis opened up the watch, and read the engraving, "Jam'elo, my love across the stars, Lena."

Francis said, "Ja'el, I don't know what to say. Thank you so much for this generous gift."

"It is no gift. It belongs to your family. We were just holding it for you."

Francis nodded. "And thank you so much for sending Jam'elo's materials to me. I plan to write a book about this whole story, and to highlight my great-great-grandmother Clara, who is well known to US history. I can't possibly imagine that being raised by a Casitian even for a few years didn't influence her life's work. I also want to research what happened to Robert Jr. There isn't much in the family history about what happened to him, since he had no children."

Ja'el replied, "I imagine such a book will be warmly received by people on both planets."

About the Author

Max has been a science fiction fan since he could read. He is a multi-genre writer, and has written and published poetry, nonfiction and technical writing. This is the fourth novel of *The Casitian Universe Series*. Max lives and works in Cazadero, CA, and Seattle, WA.

Connect with me online
Web: http://author.maxwellpearl.com